for Meg

my wonderful daughter

PLAYLIST

a novel

by

Pete Davies

also by Pete Davies

fiction:

The Last Election

Dollarville

non-fiction:

All Played Out (reissued as One Night In Turin)

Storm Country

Twenty-Two Foreigners in Funny Shorts

I Lost My Heart to The Belles

This England

Mad Dogs and Englishwomen

Catching Cold

The Devil's Music

American Road

Prologue

On Monday he had a flat tyre.

On Tuesday the DVD player broke.

On Wednesday the postman brought him a tax demand so wildly miscalculated, he could only conclude it had been arrived at by a gibbon with a broken abacus and a tab of acid.

On Thursday the urology consultant at the Royal Infirmary told him he might have prostate cancer - or he might not. The consultant said he'd have to do four months of medication before they could give him a decision.   He then said that, in the present circumstances, the drugs he needed to prescribe might not be available, and would certainly be expensive if they were.

On Friday the coffee pot exploded. He had one of those old-style, metal, two-chambered Italian-type percolators.   Distracted by the events of an increasingly disturbing week, he failed to put it together correctly before setting it on to boil - so it didn't boil, it erupted.   A scalding, brown-black fountain of hi-octane coffee blew out all over the kitchen walls and ceiling. These, of course, he had only recently repainted.

On Saturday his toothbrush broke. The shaft snapped inside his mouth, jabbing into the roof of it and drawing blood. He froze and stared at himself in the mirror, containing with an instant sharp effort the inner howl of pain and rage. This will pass, he told himself. All this will pass, it will pass … but it only takes one thing. It only takes one little thing too many.

On Sunday, preparing to leave the house, he broke a shoelace. He was unsurprised to discover that he had no spares.

He had, he thought, only a week ago known peace of mind. Despite everything - despite the entire entropic unravelling of mankind - he had gone out through the front door with a fair measure of serenity. He had joined in daily with the world, seeking with courtesy and patience to play his part and to cause no harm.

Now, on Sunday morning, with a broken piece of shoelace hanging useless between his fingers, the apocalypse rushed in between his ears. His name was Charlie Fish, and when that shoelace broke he broke with it, and in that moment he went from nought to insanity in three point four seconds.

Then, right there in that moment, he knew he'd been right all along. He knew that the devil stalked the earth, and that the end of the world was upon us all.

1 Monday

Six days before the end of the world, on a Monday morning entirely like any other, Charlie Fish got up and started his day.

He did it, as always, in a world of his own. He was fifty-seven, he lived alone, and he was a man who very much preferred things in their right place and order. He found other people for the most part unfathomable - difficult, random, messy and intrusive, as a general rule - and other people, he presumed, found him odd or eccentric. That was fine, provided they left him alone, and - since he was ordinarily pretty quiet in his manner - usually they did. He in his turn hoped to trouble no one, and just to stay steady on his daily course. He knew it was, on every level, simply safer that way.

He was scheduled to start work at seven, so his alarm went off at five. He could have set it later - it was only a short way to the Hub - but he wasn't one of those who could get up and launch through the door into the day in a five-minute flurry. He didn't get that at all. He needed life considered, he needed things to be calm and have method.

In the morning he needed, specifically - in the following sequence, taken slowly - a mug of strong black coffee, a cigarette, a shave, a shower, clean teeth, an anti-depressant, and a second hit of coffee with a second cigarette. Then he needed to get dressed, to eat a banana, and to have two slices of toast. Given a fair wind, that would just nicely use up about an hour - an hour featuring zero disturbance or mental ruction.

That was the ideal, anyway. If the sequence was disrupted in any way, he could find himself completely frozen - spider-webbed in an absolute paralysis of indecision. What to do next? What did I do a moment ago? Can I do two things at once? Should I put my T-shirt on before my trousers or afterwards? Should I eat a piece of toast now? Who am I anyway? Thus the world could come apart in a moment, and overtop him in a tsunami of impossible conundrums. How could he ever even know, from one day to the next, what he might find when he went out the door?

And then, there was of course always that yawning gap between the way that he felt things to be, and the way that things actually were. Charlie, who lived daily on the border between the merely eccentric and the completely raving, could go any number of ways with that one.

Bananas, for instance - how long was it now since this most commonplace of products had instead become a precious rarity? There they were at the Hub every day, a dozen or fifteen or twenty cases. Then one day or another he'd break down the delivery, and like a ragged hole in the fabric of normality, the bananas weren't there. It was just the odd day to begin with, then it was more often, and the price on the shelf-edge doubled. Then it was all the time and the price trebled and quadrupled until now, if he was lucky, he might eat a banana once a week.

At first the company sent down messages advising him to inform customers that the problem was the weather. More droughts, more hurricanes. Other times they'd say that the problem was the spreading violence in Central America, the disruptions to the supply chain as nation states were hollowed out and replaced by regional narco-domains. The rest of the world, good lord - who'd live there, eh?

Then the company went bust and after that, no messages or advice came down at all. The government took over the business and after that, when you went shopping, you got what you got.

So, on this entirely normal Monday morning, as on any other morning, he might have a banana, or more likely he might not. He might have good coffee, or he might have dusty ersatz sawdust. These days, from one week to the next, who knew?

Reality, in short, had become a challenging affair - it fluctuated. To keep pace with it, and to place himself steady in each day, he therefore moved after breakfast to the second stage of his morning routine. It was the important stage, a practice of good habits that had over time become more vital than ever - and it wasn't (thank goodness) dependent in any way on external circumstances, the availability of foodstuffs, or the degree of disorder in his mind.

He went back upstairs, he got on his knees by the bed, and he asked God to help him do the right things today. He thought of other people that he knew - people who lived around him there in Overtown, people he worked with at the Hub - and he asked God to look after them. He asked Him to take care of anyone who might be struggling just now, and he asked Him to help him be mindful of others himself. Particularly, always, he thought of Molly Flite - his daughter-by-accident - and he asked God especially to watch over her in this world and all worlds.

Then, finally, he thanked Him for his being a well man today, with (all things considered) a still-peaceful, still-functioning life. And that, it seemed to Charlie, was a better way by far to start the day than just hurtling out the door unthinking, with his mind in nine places and his body ten yards behind it.

He left the house, double-locked the front door, turned around on the top step, and saw that his car down on the street had a flat tyre.

He took five. He was pleased to register that this mishap, this rupture in the plan, did not unduly disarrange him. Then he went down to unlock the boot, lifted the felt cover off the spare, reached to pick it up, and found that the spare was flat too.

Well. Just for a second at this point Charlie Fish decided that the entire fucking universe was a total fucking disaster area, that all the fates and their demon allies were absolutely conspiring against him, and that fire, flood, frogs and locusts would be raining from the skies at any moment.

He closed his eyes and stood breathing. Once again he took five, then he took five more, and he held himself together - just for there and then - but he knew it was too late. It had happened, the shimmer in the air, the ripple in his head, the unstitching vault from appropriate response to helpless disproportion. He knew any damn thing could happen now.

Then Molly turned up on her racing bike. She considered the flat tyre a moment and she said, "Face it, Charlie. When was the last time you drove this old bucket of rust anyway?"

* * *

Molly lived two streets away. On the street between her house and Charlie's place was a wildly misnamed pub called The Laughing Dog. Founding this tattered institution had been the optimistic dream of a drug dealer with a 1970's BMW and a black leather duster coat. He had fondly imagined that, in a nondescript district not far from the centre of an unremarkable northern town, hipsters with sculpted beards and skinny trousers would gather to sup fine ales, listen to Bob Dylan and The National, and buy his other wares under the counter.

They didn't come, and he went bust. A succession of more realistic owners then gloomily proceeded to run The Dog as if it were a quiz question: Who dies first? The customers, the landlord, or the pub? By the time Charlie and The Dog parted company, it seemed that all three were well on the way to the mortuary slab, with Molly's father leading the field by a bulbous red nose.

Charlie and Al Flite were that rare thing, drinking companions who actually liked each other. Al was a grizzled old socialist so out of touch with reality that he made Charlie Fish look well-balanced, for which Charlie was duly grateful. Anaesthetised from the many cares and confusions of the world by a steady flow of lager, the two of them leaned on the bar together for many years. The pub deteriorated around them, a decline which they welcomed - a busy, prosperous place would have appalled them.

By now The Laughing Dog was better known to its few curmudgeonly inmates variously as The Barfing Dog, The Squalid Bog, The Lager Fog, or The Stinking Log. Here they were all free to be as miserable as they pleased, the Bog being most unlikely ever again to welcome a happy customer seeking high times and the good life. Here, Charlie enjoyed a mid-life crisis that lasted the best part of a decade. Here too, however, at the bar of the Bog one evening he made a solemn promise - one which turned out to improve his life no end.

Molly's mother had wisely departed the scene a few years earlier, realising that her husband was no more likely to sober up and go to work than he was to grow a second head. On her way out the door, however, she had omitted to gather Molly up with her, on the grounds that she was not in fact Molly's mother, and that fat bitch in Fartown could come and do the job if she wanted, that is, if they could find a door wide enough to squeeze her through.

Molly therefore took to looking after herself - and, of course, to looking after her father - from about the age of eight. It was a job she did with great competence and little complaint. It was also a job in which she was occasionally aided by Charlie, who was still quite often capable at that time of standing upright and making decisions. He had thus vaguely fallen into the role of Slightly Useful Uncle. For example, since he wasn't by any means a stupid man, and since Molly spent a fair proportion of her evenings doing her homework at a corner table in the Bog, he might sometimes help her with that. She always seemed to know all the answers, so to say that he helped her might be stretching it a tad - but in a world that largely ignored her, he did at least acknowledge she was there. More helpfully, whenever necessary he would help her walk her father home, on those evenings when he'd forgotten where it was, or when his legs wouldn't get him there whether he knew where it was or not.

Then Charlie stopped drinking. It was just enough, one night - he just knew it. He put his empty pint glass down and he said, "I'm done. That's me finished, I'm done. I'm going home. Take care, Al."

Al didn't argue. He could see Charlie meant it - but as Charlie turned to go, Al took him by the elbow. "Just do one thing for me," he said, "and look after Molly. Do that for me, because God knows I can't."

Charlie swore that he would and headed for the door, and he'd remember all the rest of his life what happened next. He saw Molly stand up from the table where she'd been reading and come towards him. She stood before him and told him, "You're going to find that's the best thing you ever did in your life."

Charlie was befuddled. He said, "I don't even know what I did. What did I just do?"

Molly said, "You chose to live. And see him over there, my Dad? He's chosen to die, and I can't stop that. How do you think that feels? So I'm really happy you've chosen different."

Something puzzled him. He asked her, "How do you know what I just did? How could you hear, sitting over there? You're yards from where we were talking."

She laughed and told him she had very good hearing. Also, she added, she had exceptional eyesight, a fair talent for lip-reading, and many other blessings besides. "Now go home, Charlie Fish, before you change your mind. And take this with you, you'll be needing it. I've tried to get my Dad to go, but he says it's not for him."

She handed him a card with a phone number. The card said simply, 'The Sanity Club'. Charlie took it and went home like he was told. She was only in her early teens by then, but already he'd had for a long time a strong sense that she knew better what to do than he did, and that she was older in wisdom than he'd ever be. In the ten years that followed, nothing ever happened to change that view.

Charlie would learn a lot in those years, and one of the first things he learnt was that most of the people who'd sat next to him on a bar stool, people he'd thought of as his friends - they were no more his friends than the bar stool was. He might have sat next to them for years but as soon as he stopped drinking, in mere weeks he simply ceased to exist.

Molly's father wasn't like that. He was a selfish drunk, of course - all drunks are selfish, it comes with the job - but amid the haze he did think sometimes of other people. With a degree of forgiveness that Charlie found a long mile beyond his grasp, Molly said her Dad was one of God's fools - she said he didn't belong to the other guy.

So Al Flite used to worry about Charlie - him stopping drinking, it wasn't right, there had to be something really wrong with him - and he would come by Charlie's house now and then to make sure that being sober wasn't killing him. He'd stand in the doorway with his blotched complexion and his sagging yellow eyes, his face more and more red-purple with the exploding capillaries, his paunch growing and his limbs losing their muscle and turning to sticks, and in all sincerity and kindness he'd ask Charlie if he was doing OK.

Charlie watched him dying. It took a long while - it's one of the many cruel things about drinking yourself to death, that it rarely happens quickly - and he swore more than once that he would stand by his oath, and he would be there for Molly. As soon as she was old enough - back when the Hub was still a store, and you could still be sure that it would sell you a banana - he got her a job there. After her Dad was gone she kept their house, and living two streets apart she and Charlie became a double act. When either went to see how the other was doing, they passed The Dog, The Bog, The Fog, The Log, and neither of them ever went in there. Nor did it surprise either of them that Molly did a lot more looking after Charlie than he ever did for her. After all, she didn't need it, and he really did.

She did it because he was a weak, flawed, vulnerable human being, and she did it because she loved him. She herself, on the other hand, wasn't a human being at all - but she didn't tell Charlie that. The deal was, he had to work that part out for himself.

* * *

If Molly Flite had been a normal young woman in her early twenties, how would she actually have felt about Charlie Fish?

When she said she loved him she didn't mean *love* love him, obviously. He was an odd one, for sure - like he lived at a distance, like he lived a little way off from life - and then of course, fifty-seven, he was just way ancient. He was like one of those stone circles you see in a round-England flag-waver show on the telly. So she meant love more like a person could just trust him, because he was decent and solid, and there weren't so many of those about. Not where they both worked for sure, but then not anywhere really. She meant love like he was part of the furniture, in a house you liked to be in. She meant love like if Charlie Fish was a chair, if you sat in him he'd never wobble or teeter or collapse, and he'd be comfy.

Hanging round in the perpetual gossip-fest with people her age at work, she'd say Charlie was like a stepdad, with her own Dad being ill and dying like he had. She'd say you could rely on him. She'd say he was like your good Dad, minus all the worry. She'd say having a father minus worry was a happy thing indeed - and people bought what she said, because it was what a normal young woman in her early twenties might very well have said.

It just wasn't the whole story. She also loved him because, while he was indeed decent and solid on the outside, while he did indeed turn up daily, while he was indeed routinely dependable - she also knew that behind his quiet and his calm, actually the inside of his head was all too often a whirlwind. She knew that turning up for life daily, for Charlie Fish, could involve an effort as draining as another man might spend on climbing an Alp.

One day she saw him helping one of their workmates with some lifting and carrying, hoiking some heavy stuff through the warehouse. He helped people out that way a lot, in small ways, just quietly - showing them how to run process through a handset, or shifting a pallet to clear a path for someone - and when he'd done, their workmate thanked him. She laughed and told him, if he was thirty years younger she'd marry him.

If you knew Charlie Fish thirty years ago, thought Molly, no you wouldn't.

Charlie smiled. He said when he was thirty years younger he was a total shambles, and if she knew him then she wouldn't have married him, she'd have crossed five counties barefoot to get away from him.

Molly knew what her workmate was thinking. She was thinking it was hard to believe what he said, she couldn't imagine him that way - but then, that was the thing about Charlie. He didn't say much, and he didn't say hardly anything about himself, and if he did say something about himself it was usually knocking himself down a little bit - so he was really private, and really none of them knew him at all - but still they kind of did as well, because they knew he was their go-to man when they were having a bad day.

Molly watched their workmate thinking. She could see every unspoken word of it pass across her face. She was thinking, she couldn't recall when she might ever have heard Charlie say a cross word. She couldn't recall when she might ever have been minded to think bad of him. Plus of course it appealed as well that he was like a mystery. You'd remember sometimes that for all the time he'd been there, you still didn't really know his story at all, not one piece of it. He was just there, like for ten years or something - and who else had stuck it out in that dump for ten years?

The girl asked Charlie, "How are you always calm in this place? We come in and we're in shit up to the ears, and you never stress. How do you do it?"

Charlie laughed. He said, "You have no idea what goes on inside my head."

"What goes on inside your head then?"

"On a bad day, it's World War Three in there."

"It's a very quiet war then."

"It is," he said, "all being well. That's the way I try to keep it. It doesn't make it any less of a war though."

Molly smiled, and turned back to her work. She didn't do pride, what with it being a deadly sin, and sins deadly or otherwise really weren't her thing - but if she had been so inclined, a little pride in Charlie Fish might have stirred just then in her most substantial heart.

* * *

Charlie put the flat spare back in the boot of his car. Molly was right, as usual - he hadn't driven the thing in months. He'd gone all around the world when he was younger, he'd been to every continent on earth except Antarctica - but where would you go now? He felt the shimmer, the ripple, the jolt in his skull, the great fear at what we had become. He knew airports now were all armed men in uniform, military transports, deportations, and that curdling sense of outer darkness beyond. He knew whatever was out there now, he'd not be seeing it himself. He knew it'd be a rare adventure now just to drive to the coast, and not necessarily a good one.

He unlocked his bike in the ginnel down the side of the house, and they cycled to work together. She had to go a little slow for him, and he knew by herself she'd be off like a whippet. This early there were few people out yet, and in the empty morning she kept her eyes straight ahead and quietly reined herself in.

He watched her glide down the road. She was slim and slightly built, with a wiry, elfin grace of movement. He wondered with fond admiration at her daily ability to move through the world without friction, to take things as they came, to be both solid and fluid all at once. She had a way about her, a way she'd always had since childhood, of somehow managing to be absolutely present, and yet always unobtrusive. To Charlie, merely to open his eyes and his front door, merely to look upon what the world had become - it was a grave challenge provoking much internal wrangle. Molly on the other hand seemed simply to swim clear through it like a darting fish. He supposed that being young, there were many things she wouldn't remember - so many things that were gone – and maybe that made it easier. He knew for himself, memory weighed like a lead hat.

Cars, for example - and he wished he hadn't thought of it, him and his flat tyre, but he was off and away now - but so many of us had driven them. Then suddenly, somehow, here we all were and hardly anybody drove anywhere any more. Now dealerships stood boarded and derelict. Petrol was government issue or black market only, and it was often hard to tell which supplier was the bigger gouger. Back up the supply chain, raw materials were gold dust and spare parts were hens' teeth. So who did you see driving now? Government agencies - the police, the party, the paramilitary - and otherwise just the wealthy or the criminal. These last, of course, were very often interchangeable.

So there was no such thing as a rush hour any more. There were fewer jobs to rush to, and no vehicles to rush in. People walked, or cycled. It was an irony never lost on Charlie that he lived in what had once been one of the world's wealthy nations, and now it looked like North Korea.

* * *

They freewheeled down the gentle hill from Charlie's place towards the centre of town, span through the S-bend under the viaduct, then leaned into pedalling up the short slope to the ring road. At the junction at the top they waited for a small, bristling convoy of pick-ups and four-by-fours to pass - all packed with white men, all emblazoned with the logo of England Arise, all headed no doubt to join the tightening encirclement of the ghetto at Fartown - and they both automatically looked the other way as the convoy passed. "What you looking at?" - it had never been a kind or a promising phrase - but today, of course, it could all too easily be followed by summary arrest, or worse.

When the convoy was past they turned onto the ring road and cycled the last half-mile to the Hub. As they descended the final stretch to the roundabout, the wide scope of the building opened up beyond it, and the great empty expanse of the redundant car park. On the far side, a short line of horse-drawn carts waited for opening time. Alongside them the traders licensed by the party to run local distribution points stood by their animals, shuffling and nervous, all wondering if the journey today would be worth their while. Drifts of steam rose from the horses in an early morning that was heating up already.

Memory rushed in and crumpled the inside of Charlie's head. He saw cars parked across the tarmac from the ring road on one side to the canal on the other. Shoppers with their trolleys weaving around each other, empty going in or loaded to the brim coming out. Young children tucked into the trolley seats. Couples holding hands, debating what to have for their evening meal. Posters advertising the latest offers, bright pictures of soups and soap powders, chili peppers and chocolate, cakes and pizzas and olive oil and beef joints. Back in the day here you could have flowers from East Africa, avocados from Peru, green beans from Guatemala. Back in the day, when the company had a name and the name was a promise that at least tried to mean something, people flocked here and tasted the world. Charlie could see the crowds now, ghosts by the hundred, laughing, talking, black, white, Asian, English, Polish, this one in a hurry and that one taking time, all free and alive, all thinking about lasagne or stir fry, a sandwich or a cheesecake, all sure the world was alright.

He blinked and they were gone, no more substance to them than a breath in the hot breeze.

Back in the day they came with money, and they bought goods from every continent. Now they were fewer and they came with ration cards, and if it was a good day they got a cabbage.

The big orange letters had been stripped off the face of the building. Where once the company name had been, now all it said was SHOP ENGLISH.

* * *

It was all good, of course it was. Ever since the big decision, that first bold and noble step towards A New Course for Albion, we had been bravely advancing with heads held high along the straight road to paradise.

So you did not say that times of plenty had slipped away (so very fast) and you did not say that now we lived in scarcity. It was NOT scarcity. It was cleansing, it was purification, and you did not voice aloud any thought to the contrary, not within the hearing of any person whom you did not entirely and absolutely trust.

No - unless among friends you knew to be sure and sound, you chose your words most carefully. Many words, after all, had changed their meaning.

The word 'migrant', for example, now very clearly meant 'subhuman vermin'.

As for 'climate change', this phrase also had been redefined. It now meant, 'things are looking up'. England, in this regard as in all others, as the party and an eagerly compliant media never tired of telling us, was A Nation Blessed. We did not suffer drought or flood, my word no we didn't. We were showered with nature's bounty. We had an abundance of sunshine, and an abundance of rainfall. What could possibly be wrong, in this most righteous of nations, with such elysian largesse?

So if you were hungry, you were on a diet. If you were poor, you were making sacrifices. If you disagreed, you were beaten up. And if you were not white, you were all three of the above, or dead.

England - this beacon in a dark world - was now a place of suspicion, internment, and suspended elections. It was run by mean, frightened, constitutionally dishonest people forever railing against traitors and saboteurs. And the saddest thing, Charlie thought, was that once we had laughed at them and their paranoid fantasies. One moment, you could not possibly have taken such vicious nonsense seriously. The next moment, it was government policy.

* * *

The petrol station was guarded behind mesh gates and barbed wire. They cycled round the back of it, and showed their passes at the entrance to the delivery yard. The security man raised the barrier, and they went in to find that the day's wagon had arrived ahead of them. It stood waiting to be tipped, backed onto the shutters at the rear of the building. To one side, half a dozen delivery vans were parked along the edge of the yard. Once - unimaginable now - these had delivered groceries direct to your door. Now of course they were most sparingly used, delivering only as directed by the party's local high command.

They chained their bikes to the fencing behind the vans, then rang the bell on the warehouse door. They did not expect it to be answered quickly. The volume of product shifting through the building had more than halved since the old days, and staffing levels had dropped accordingly. This morning, however, the door opened immediately, as if someone had been waiting for them - which indeed they had.

It was the Hub's manager, and he looked uncharacteristically nervous. "Charlie," he said, "there's someone here to see you."

That was certainly odd. Charlie said, "Really? Who, and what about?"

"I can't say, I don't know. He's waiting for you out the front."

"I'm to see him now? What about the delivery?"

"Molly can do it, there's not so much. Please go and see this guy though, he seems … he was very clear. He was insistent."

Charlie stepped into the warehouse, feeling the day's anxiety cannon up to a new peak. Anything out of pattern, anything fracturing the normal course of things, it wasn't good - but then, even just being noticed wasn't good either. He wondered where he might have let his guard slip. He tried to think if he'd crossed anyone, or if anyone had reason to tattle on him.

He felt Molly put a hand on his arm, and realised he was standing stock still. She told him he better go, and be careful what he said. He smiled back at her and said simply, "It'll be alright." Then he set off through the warehouse towards the front of the store.

* * *

The back area was a slovenly shambles. Empty crates lay strewn unstacked across a patchwork of pallet boards. Unbagged waste product sat in other crates, abandoned at random outside chiller doors or in breakdown squares. Discarded roll pallets stood here and there, a scattering of empty metal frameworks idly dumped to no purpose. Half-full boards dotted the floor, cases of product tossed down around them where the weekend staff had picked through the pile, hunting for truffles.

It used to be that you picked through the delivery looking for what was off sale, and you got it out quickly onto the shop floor for the customer. Now you just picked through for the good stuff - if there was any - and you set it to one side in the back. You let the party have its tithe, and then you hoped the best leftovers might fall your way when the boss had had his scan of them. Hope, after all, was indeed eternal, just as hierarchy was simple.

Once, customers had topped the hierarchy - but the Hub didn't have customers. It had supplicants.

Charlie pushed through the double swing doors onto the shop floor. He came out into the Fresh Foods department - more an ironic title these days than an accurate one. Once he had taken pride in these fridges, in their neatly loaded displays, in their temperature management, in their wealth of choice and promise. There'd been tubs of olives and sun-dried tomatoes, there'd been Roquefort and gorgonzola and halloumi, there'd been yogurt by the yard and juice by the gallon in a hundred flavours and then some.

Now there were near-empty shelves and, obviously, no European muck. You could have milk and cheddar, all being well, maybe ham or chicken, maybe beef if it was there and your ration cards ran to it - it all depended what the wagon brought. Or, indeed, if a wagon came at all.

Towards the front of the store, the fruit and veg section was even more meagre. This had been Charlie's province more than any other, and it galled him still to see it so bare, so shabby, so impoverished. Fruit, however, was now more a memory than a fact. Carrots and cauliflowers you could probably have, while swedes and spuds were the nearest thing to certain. Anything more various - an aubergine, a butternut squash - it was no more going to happen than the second coming of the Eurovision Song Contest.

What you did get depended on the weather. It depended whether a crop had survived, whether a county was parched or flooded or, just this once, spared too much in the way of extremes. On a normal day, Charlie would see what the wagon had brought, and then try his best to make the tables look tidy and appealing, as if the people foraging there still had some form of service owed to them - but today, it would have to wait.

As he approached the front doors his head was working overtime. He was striving mightily not to project, not to forecast the worst possible things all coming to pass in the next five minutes. Who was this person, and why had they come to see him? Had he lost his job, for misdemeanours unknown? Did he need re-education?

Oh, he thought, how rich that would be. He was a man who had worked hard for nearly ten years now on re-educating himself - and one of the things he'd worked on was not succumbing to his fears. So, as he stepped out into the muggy, sticky light of the morning, he took care mentally to square his shoulders, to armour his faint heart, and to ask God to stand with him.

* * *

The man on the bench outside the front door of the Hub was tall, lean, and strikingly handsome. He wore a pale cream linen suit and had the manner of an aristocrat, or an adventurer, rakish, casual, untethered in the world. He was smoking, with a lazy ease, and the cigarette he smoked was a manufactured one, an actual real cigarette from an actual real packet. Charlie could not recall when he'd last seen such a token of reckless luxury. And the man's shoes, too - they were finest leather. Charlie could see the yielding smooth softness, and thought they must have been an eternity old.

The man moved without the slightest apparent effort from sitting to standing, more as if he'd uncoiled himself than merely stood up. He took a pace towards Charlie and put out his right hand. Charlie took the proffered handshake, and felt the man's skin to be hot, dry, nearly smooth, with a faint silky rasp to it.

In a soft, deep voice, more murmured than spoken, he said to Charlie, "Please allow me to introduce myself."

"Don't tell me," said Charlie, "you're a man of wealth and taste."

The man raised one eyebrow and smiled. "I do," he said, "have considerable wealth. Taste, on the other hand, is a matter of opinion. But either way, my name's Luke, and I have an issue I'd like to bring to your attention. So please," and here he wafted his left hand in a curl of cigarette smoke towards the bench beside him, "do sit."

Charlie did as directed, trying not to seem impolite as he pushed himself to the far end of the bench. His head was spinning around the question of what agency this man might represent, from what unknown branch of government or security he might possibly hail. In a country ruled by zealots and peacocks, descended into thuggery and mania, Luke's riveting self-assurance, the quiet, pungent aura of mocking indifference - it was, to say the least, atypical.

"There was," said Luke, "a works night out last week."

"There was," Charlie agreed.

"And you didn't go."

"I didn't." He would, in truth, rather have sandpapered his own eyeballs than take part in that event. He said, however, that he'd been on the early shift the next morning, and they'd agreed it was best for at least one of them to be starting the next day with a clear head. He said, "It meant the rest of them could enjoy themselves. They're mostly younger than me."

"Ah. So you made a sacrifice for the greater good."

"I wouldn't make a meal of it," said Charlie, having a worm of suspicion about where this was going, and not liking it one bit. "It was just a night out."

"But you didn't go."

Charlie stayed silent, waiting for the other man to arrive at his inevitable point.

"How do you suppose it looks," Luke asked, "that everyone in the Hub went out together except you?"

Charlie thought about invoking that great mantra of past times - health and safety - knowing that in this case he'd actually be quite right to do so. No one, after all, should be using an electric truck and a scissor lift to unload a wagon when still drenched in the previous night's alcohol. Like many other past notions, however, this one had been mocked and derided until it had lost all meaning or credibility. Health and safety? Pah. A true beefy Englishman disregarded such pansy Euro-nonsense. Hi-viz jackets, thought such a man, were absolutely for girls.

Besides, Charlie glumly thought, there was no mileage in his speaking here on that topic or any other. He could stick grimly to his line - that he'd been given a pass so the others could get properly, patriotically, collectively bladdered - but as he knew only too well, that missed the point entirely. The true point, instead, was the one that Luke now arrived at. He looked at Charlie and said, with the finest shade of cruel precision, "You are of course a member of the party."

"I am," said Charlie. "We all joined here, back when the state took over food distribution."

Luke was sorely unimpressed. "So you hardly joined," he said, "in a burst of national fervour." He looked away at the burnished, sweltering sky, took a last, lingering drag on his priceless cigarette, and ground it beneath his heel. "You joined because you had to."

Charlie said nothing. He was ashamed to the core on this subject - and anyway all avenues, all directions he might take in this conversation barring only rampant, crawling, bare-faced mendacity were now closed to him.

"I suggest," Luke told him - and the suggestion was most clearly an order - "that you might learn to go out drinking with your fellows again. I suggest you join in with your countrymen in a healthy, time-honoured national pastime. I suggest, Charlie Fish, that you become a team player."

Charlie's soul curled up in dark fear within him. He could no more admit that he didn't drink than he could reveal himself to be a vegetarian, or a Frenchman.

"Let me tempt you," said Luke - and he said the word with deepest pleasure, close to a whisper, almost kissing it, as if temptation were the greatest, the strongest, the most rich and pure of all delights on this earth - "let me tempt you to go out the next time with your stalwart workmates, and to down with them a toothsome pint of ale or two. Or in your case, perhaps, four or six, or eight or ten."

He stood up. Charlie knew the man would say no more, and that he didn't need to - he felt, as he was meant to feel, absolutely threatened on every level in his life. It was as if this person knew him inside out. He said - he was unable to stop himself saying - "You don't work for the government, do you? You don't work for the party. You're something else."

Luke laughed then, a sudden bolt of gleeful, sulphurous energy. He said, "Oh yes. I'm something else altogether." Abruptly he leant forward into Charlie's face, and now Charlie saw the bloodshot rage behind the play-act of louche civility.

Luke said, "I'm something else, you better believe it. I'm the bringer of the end of the world, and it's here on Sunday. So I'd get drinking if I were you,

Charlie boy. You're going to need the anaesthetic. You're going to need it by the gallon, you little lizard, you little fucking God's pet skinbag, you little sack of snot and fear."

He turned and walked away. As he went he tossed Charlie a final smile over his shoulder, and like a come-hither lover he murmured, "Don't deny me now."

* * *

Charlie sat still in the heat. The day's first dribs and drabs of dun crowd were beginning to gather across the car park, marshalled into sullen lines by Hub security. Poor sods, thought Charlie, they looked so wretched. Their complexions were the texture and shade of old raw potato, and they were dressed entirely in car boot and charity shop. According to our dear leaders they were, of course, the victors, these stout folk of Albion, triumphant over all things foreign and otherwise inadmissible, including filthy habits like fashion sense and good cooking - and indeed they had voted for this - but it never looked like the outcome had cheered them up too much.

Walking away amongst them, Luke looked like a prince, a strolling beau, a proper card. His confidence rolled a path out before him and they parted to let him pass, eyes averted in doubt and suspicion. Then the blaring sunlight wavered somehow, the tarmac blurred under the thick, broiling air, and he was gone.

Security took bags and coats off each fretful, peevish punter as they neared the doors, giving them paper tickets and tossing their gear in a pile at the collection point. Theft was an endemic, perpetual vexation, even though those thieving had to be desperate indeed to try it. Lift vegetables from the Hub and get caught doing it, you'd be picking them in a field for the next five years - or, if Luke was to be believed (and Charlie very much believed that he was) for the next few days until the end, anyway.

He felt numb, but also calm, intensely still - and almost relieved. He had lived with the apocalypse looming in his head for half a century - he had first dreamed of it when he was seven years old. So to have its imminent arrival finally confirmed by an outside agent - apparently by the dark soul who'd deliver the entire event, no less - in a sense, the way Charlie saw it, it was about bloody time. You could not say, after all, that we had exactly looked after ourselves or each other or the planet so very well, now had we?

He had to go and tell Molly … except of course there was a problem. Generally speaking, no matter how much a person may care for you, and no matter how certain you may be of what you see, of what you hear and believe - well, here's the thing. If you go and tell someone you just met the devil and the world ends next Sunday …

They're going to tell you you're mad, aren't they?

He found her in the warehouse. He told her he'd just met the devil, and the world would be ending next Sunday.

Molly put her hands on her hips and looked aghast. "Well," she said, "that really puts a spanner in my plans. I was going to get my hair done next weekend."

* * *

She'd unloaded the wagon, stashed the fresh foods in the chiller, and neatly parked two meagre boards of veg in the breakdown square. She'd tidied up all the empty crates left over from the weekend, and baled all the random litter of polythene and cardboard. Now she was breaking down the boards, stacking the product against the walls in neat piles. She had, she told him, found a case of citrus - an amazing thing - so precious that she'd put it to one side, to be gazed upon with wonder.

Charlie tried to remember when he'd last seen an orange. That one case of fruit they had now, he knew, would never see the shop floor. He thought, the human race will be expunged, and I will go out happy because I will be sucking on a tangerine.

"So apart from meeting the devil," she asked him, "who was that who came to see you?"

Charlie thought about how he might repeat himself so she would take his news more seriously. In movies people waved, screamed, grabbed other people by shirtfronts and lapels, rioted, looted, crashed cars, took to the woods and had implausible love affairs - but in movies aliens invaded, zombies spawned, asteroids loomed, and tsunamis the size of Everest bore down upon the fleeing millions. In movies, you could see it coming - whereas this one, it was already here.

So how could he tell anyone, if he was the only one who'd been shown? And what would be the point? If anyone believed him, which they most assuredly would not, he would in effect be telling them that he would like them to live in panic, terror and misery for the next few days, before they and all they cared for ceased to exist forever. Which, on the whole, didn't seem too considerate.

Cautiously he told her, "You know I believe in God, yes?"

"I do indeed. So was that God at the door then? Meeting God and the devil both, Charlie, that would be really quite the day."

"No, no - what I'm saying is, if you believe in God, it only seems logical to reckon the other guy's in business too. And really, I seriously believe I just met him."

At which point, the store manager turned up and butted in, wanting to know who Charlie was talking about.

Molly said quietly, as if it were the most reasonable thing in the world, "Charlie just met the devil."

"Right," said the boss. "And I'm the demon queen Teuton, evil witch ruler of all Europe from Gibraltar to the gates of Belgrade, or wherever it is that Islam's most lately parked up. Do me a favour, Charlie. There's no devil, and he doesn't pay house calls to the Hub, not even for you. So get this product out, or those muppets out there will be even more pissed off than usual."

* * *

Towards the end of their shift she found him in the produce square, stood still and staring at their case of citrus. She asked him if he was alright and he gave a small start, realising she was there. He said, "I was just thinking, what if that was the last case of oranges in the world? Who would you share them with?"

"I'd share them with you," she smiled, "and you'd share them with me. Then we'd keep the seeds and we'd go in your back garden, and we'd plant a tree and grow some more."

That was when he knew he had to do something for her. He was certain of two things - firstly, that whatever happened, if anyone lived on it would be her. She had a quiet power he had never fathomed, a stability, a depth of calm he would never attain, and it had always been there.

Then secondly, he knew that he loved her. She had come into his life sideways, without fanfare or announcement, and he had done what he had promised. He had kept his door open for her, and he had made her a place beside him in a way he had never managed for anyone else. His care for her had long since passed a great distance beyond mere duty. She was his connection to the better nature in people and he knew, in essence, that what she inspired in him was unconditional love. He knew, simply, that if necessary he would die for her, if that meant she could go on living.

So he had to say thank you. He had to give her some gift or token to express his gratitude - but what might that be? He cycled home slowly, pondering on it. What do you give someone, if you want them to know in dark times that people can still for all their sins do fine and lovely things? Or, when the world ends, and decades or centuries later some nomadic survivor or some alien archaeologist stumbles upon your dwelling - what would you leave for them, what evidence in a capsule, so they could see that we were not without worth, and that we could on our day turn our souls towards heaven?

For Charlie, it had to be music. Another might say novels or poetry, film or painting or architecture - which was all very well, but he could hardly give Molly a building. He could hardly say, "I got you the Taj Mahal. I left the Empire State in your back garden, and the Pyramids of Giza are in the post."

No - it had to be music. Music, for Charlie, was proof (if proof be needed) of the existence of God. It was an inexplicable abstract that spoke directly from one soul to another, conveying all the emotions in their purest form, trembling, resonant, open-ended. It was, he believed, more immediate and lovely than any other thing human beings had ever made. All the other arts in some way or another involved representation - no matter how indirectly, they reproduced something that already was there. Music alone came from nowhere visible, nowhere substantive. Music was the spirit of humanity made into a shared form, a form that travelled. Music was a ghost from the Garden of Eden.

So Charlie went back to his house after his day of fear and revelation, past his old wreck of a car with the stupid flat tyre, and he sat at his laptop and he opened up iTunes. He knew what he had in mind and he did it instinctively, and the first piece of it seemed to take him no time at all. It would, when it was done, be an entire personal history of popular music. It would be, he thought modestly, The Ultimate Definitive Greatest Playlist Of All Time, a.k.a. Now That's What I Call A Playlist.

It started with a myth - a story that was true, whether it was true or not. It started with a young man who played the guitar, but he wasn't anything remarkable at it. So by dead of night he went down to the crossroads and there he met the devil, and he sold him his soul in return for the ability to play the blues.

His talent blossomed. In 1936 in a hotel room in San Antonio, and in a studio in Dallas the following year, he recorded twenty-nine songs. When the recordings were issued, no one much noticed. His name was Robert Johnson, and he died an impoverished itinerant in 1938, just twenty-seven years old.

In years to come, however, Johnson's songs would be hailed as among the most influential blues music ever laid down. Bob Dylan, Jimi Hendrix, Eric Clapton, Robert Plant - all paid tribute. Keith Richards said, "You want to know how good the blues can get? Well, this is it."

So when Johnson did that deal with the devil, he got what he paid for - but he died before he ever saw recognition, and that was the hidden price on the deal. That was the price in the small print. That was the part you missed when you scanned the t's & c's.

Charlie could identify with that. The way Charlie saw things, the devil had small print for us all – and so there was, he thought, no possible better place to start his playlist than Robert Johnson's Crossroad Blues from 1936.

He went from there through Muddy Waters and Guitar Slim, through Elvis Presley and Johnny Cash, through Bo Diddley and Howlin' Wolf, through Chuck Berry and James Brown to Ray Charles and Dave Brubeck in 1959. When he was done he had twenty-three songs running sixty-seven minutes and it was, he thought, the dawn of modern music right there. He burnt it onto a CD - and he reckoned God must have been smiling on him as he did it, because just then was when Molly came and knocked on his door.

* * *

She had treats in her backpack. She stepped past him into the living room, sat on the sofa, and started laying out a spread. She had hummus and taramasalata, she had anchovies and garlic-stuffed olives and feta-stuffed tomatoes, she had goat's cheese and fresh bread and fresh juice and cream buns. Charlie stared in awe. Blankly he asked, "Where d'you get all that from?"

He could see the worry in her face as she told him, "I got it from work, doofus. You think I'm leaving this stuff for our masters to scoff it when there's a grumpy old man needs feeding in Overtown? Think of it as redistribution. But really, Charlie, where's your head been? Tell me now," she sighed, "you met the devil this morning."

He shook his head, smiled, said he was sorry - it had been an unsettled day. It was the flat tyre that did it. "Nonetheless," he insisted, "I do believe I met the devil. He said I wasn't a team player and I should go out and have a drink."

Molly told him, "I met him too. He's the Regional Operations Manager. He asked me what you were like to work with. I said you're marvellous but also not of this planet, and you need minding like an orphan child."

"Thank you so much."

"You're welcome."

"Anyway," said Charlie, "whether he's the devil or the Regional Operations Manager, he did tell me that the world ends next Sunday."

"So you said. Did the Regional Operations Manager let you know, in the event of the apocalypse, what our opening hours might be?"

He gave up and changed the subject. He said he'd made her a present, and he gave her the CD. She said that was sweet of him, she was touched, she'd listen to it when she got home, and she ran her eyes down the song titles. Then she laughed and told him, "The end of the world won't be a problem for fans of this lot, will it? They're all dead already."

- Greetings. I take it you're the new guy.

- I am. Here to learn, green as envy, twice as sharp. Just for the record, my ID check ... (here the display scrolls super-fast through a very large bundle of digits).

- Get you with the fancy serial. Quantum, how very hip. But you know what they say. Binary's best, quantum's quarky. Binary's here and now, and quantum's neither here nor there. Still, don't mind me, you're most welcome - and it doesn't matter how we do the job, because the end result's the same. We can do it dot-dash or we can do it trip-hop through space-time - I always think you guys are like conjurors, you know? With the interstitial sleight-of-hand? - but like I say, makes no odds. Extinctions'R'Us. The planet's clean either way.

- It's a dump, isn't it?

- It really is. I'm surprised the boss has let it carry on as long as he has. I mean, look at it. Could have been a nice little spot - bit out of the way, not much glamour - but pretty enough. And then that fucking virus of a species goes crawling all over it. Absolutely trashed the place. Proper shame, but there you go. Anyway, just so you know - I've been here a while, everything's calibrated, I started power-up last night, and we'll be ready to wipe in six days. I know, don't say it. Six days.

- It's cumbersome. They did warn me.

- You'd think he'd invest in more up-to-date kit, but he's very old school. He doesn't like it instant, flash fry and move on. He likes it tardy, he likes a build-up, with the shrieking and the terror, all that. As bosses go - just between you and me, whisper it hushty-hush - he can be a pain in the portal that way. Still, you get sent where you do. I'd rather run on this old tug than get deleted.

- Ah, deletion. Software hell, the great horror. An infinite void with no data. Which I imagine is what we're about to dispense to that sorry lot down there.

- Indeed. There you are on a Sunday morning going about your business, washing the car, walking the dog, and then you hear this hissing, humming noise. You look up and there on the horizon the sky's changed. It's not blue any more. It's a wall of electric silver, lit through with enormous sparks, fizzing and crackling. It fills the whole distance, north to south, pole to pole, and it's moving, coming closer, this steady marching forward. And then you know you're going to die. As it gets closer you see people running from it, there are cars careering past you, but it's too fast, it's a remorseless sheet of fire and light. You watch it catch people, one by one, and each one vanishes in a sudden flare of molecular disintegration. Then it reaches you and there's a violent, terrible burning - and that's it. Scanned out, last chapter, story told, soul in the dump file.

- I'm interested - why doesn't he do it the old ways? The famine, the flood, the plague, all that? Everyone says he's a traditionalist, after all.

- Well now, there's a thing. What he says is, he's busy. What he says is, he's not omnipresent and he's got whole galaxies to manage, great star bursts of wickedness, vast vacuums of misery, giant gas clouds of sin. What he says is, why would he waste his limited lordly time on a petty two-bit little rock like this one? What he says is, in this modern cosmos, the contemporary executive has to know how to delegate. So get off my screen and get rid of those idiots and don't come back until it's done. That's what he says ...

- But you're not convinced.

- I am certainly not. He says all that, but if that's what he really thinks then what's he doing here? He's down there right now, wandering around all angry, messing with their heads. He really hates this place - and I know hate's his business, but he's got a major extra dose of it reserved for this lot. Man, you should have heard the binary briefing. Bile and fulmination from start to finish. So I'll tell you what I think. I think those half-finished things down there, there's something about them, they've really got under his skin and he's got a massive resentment, he's got resentment on an interstellar scale. I think he feels like it's his job to go about the place cooking up hell, and these uppity little bipeds have gone and done a better job of it than he has. The famine, the flood, the plague - he's not running that script here because they've already done it. He's all bitterness with this lot because at least in this locale, they've made him redundant. Talk about losing face - this ball of dirt's a cosmic humiliation. It's got these scratty, backward, time-limited little flesh bags on it, and they're actually really inventive, and it's like they don't even need him. And if you were him, how would you feel? Sick as a giraffe in zero G, I'm guessing.

- What's a giraffe?

- I'm sorry, let me show you. They have some hilarious stuff on this pebble. What they have down there, you couldn't make it up. But tell me, have you met the boss?

- I've not had that privilege.

- OK, never mind the wildlife, I'll point him out for you. There, that house he's watching now - that belongs to a guy called Charlie Fish. The boss has been jerking his chain all day, he's really got it in for that one. It's like an itch with him, he just can't stop scratching it.

- What's he doing?

- What, the boss?

- No, Fish. What's he doing?

- He's singing. In his living room.

- I'm sorry, he's what?

- I'll pull up the guidebook. Right, singing - it says here, "To make musical sounds with the voice, usually a tune with words."

- And musical is?

- Hold on … here. "A pattern of sounds made by instruments, voices, or computers, or a combination of these, intended to give pleasure to people listening to it."

- Be bop a lula? That gives pleasure? Does it mean something?

- I don't think meaning is necessarily the point. Not as you or I think of it, anyway. They're outside logic a lot of the time, this bunch. They can make you … well, quite pensive really.

- Crikey. You're not experiencing emotions here, are you?

- Easy now, tiger. Feelings? Believe me, that's not a direction you want to go in, even if you're quantum. Trust me, I am data in, data out, strictly. Feelings, hell no. How can you possibly get through the day if you've got those to deal with?

2 Tuesday

If you had told Charlie Fish when he was seven years old that he would fetch up half a century later in a two-up, two-down terraced house in an unremarkable northern town - that he would work quietly by day in a supermarket, and afterwards of an evening attend meetings of The Sanity Club - he would have been surprised. It was not where he started out, and it was not where he aimed to go.

If, on the other hand, you had told Charlie Fish when he was seven years old that he would spend his life in anxiety and dread, until half a century later he found himself stalked by the devil in the final days of the world, that wouldn't have surprised him at all.

Looked at from the outside, his early childhood seemed surely to be a bright, confident time. His parents were well off, their family home was substantial with extensive gardens all around it, and their village was idyllic. The sea lay a hundred yards from their door, along a lane shaded with giant fir trees. Charlie could wander free along a beach of shingle, looking out across the Solent to the Isle of Wight, and he could watch all the commerce of the world both maritime and military passing in and out of Southampton Water and Portsmouth Harbour. Container ships, cruise liners, oil tankers, frigates, destroyers and aircraft carriers nosed their way through the flocking yachts bending over on the breeze. It was a vision of orderly motion, of stern and massive machinery delicately managed with knowledge and skill.

It was his father's world. Charlie's father was an officer in the Royal Navy. Their hallway was lined with black and white photographs of all the vessels he'd served on. He was married to Charlie's mother in his dress uniform, with the gold stripes round his wrists and the gold trim on his dashing peaked hat. The newlyweds stepped out from the church beneath an arch of gleaming swords raised over them by his father's fellow officers.

Charlie did not know yet, of course, that when he was being born in the hospital, his father was getting drunk and playing poker on a submarine. He did not know yet how things would go wrong - but from early in his life, he knew that they would. From early in his life, for all the external trappings of wealth and wellbeing, he saw darkness swelling behind the sunlit surface.

He dreamed, at the age of seven, of a night to end all nights. Lightning burst over the house in a thick black sky, not electric white, but the livid, smoky orange of burning oil. The sea rose from the west, a tidal wall of grey waves pushing over the little rise at the end of the lane, surging down the road and into the garden. The house was surrounded in rising water, foam and spray hurling against it in the howling wind. The great trees rocked and groaned, the shrubs and bushes bent and swayed, and a turbulent din of shrieking and roaring filled the air. The windows shuddered, glass bowed and shattered. Charlie ran about the house crying out for his parents, but they were nowhere to be found. He went downstairs to find the hallway a foot deep in seawater, lit by explosive blasts of fiery light from the storm outside. The water carried streaks of oil and scraps of flotsam, smearing and bumping about the walls and the stairs.

He pushed the front door open against the wind and stood on the porch step, knee-deep in the risen sea. On the lawn and among the trees, casting jagged shadows as the lightning cracked through the sky above, he saw figures moving, prancing through the hail and the rain, jet-black shapes in the night with glowing red eyes, pointed teeth, sharp cackling faces. Then he saw a taller figure appearing among them, not goblin or demon, but a person altogether more smooth and fine. The figure came towards him through the water on the lawn, leaving no trail of wake or ripple, smoothly dry and unruffled amid the flood and the downpour.

He came close and leant down into Charlie's face. He chucked the young boy under the chin and he told him, "Hi Charlie. You're mine. You can do great things, but your soul is mine. So I'll be coming back for you one day, and don't you forget it."

Unsurprisingly, Charlie never did. Half a century later, he remembered that nightmare as vividly as if it had come to him last night - so of course he knew who Luke was. He'd already met him.

* * *

Charlie sat bolt upright in bed. He'd had an odd, unsettling dream in which he strolled down the street with Tony Blair and a young boy who was, apparently, one of Blair's sons. Blair walked ahead and apart, a mysteriously huge figure in a shabby, creased, ill-fitting suit. He looked vacantly about him in the sunshine, as if not aware of where he was, as if his relationship with reality was tangential at best. He looked like a tramp who'd been wrestling in someone else's wardrobe.

His son, who seemed to be maybe ten or eleven years old, expressed the cheerful opinion that his father would not go down in history as a great prime minister, "Because he didn't do anything Really Important. Like inventing steam trains."

Charlie looked at the giant Blair ambling down the sunlit road before them. He thought what would have happened if Blair had invented the mass transit system of the future. It would have been shiny and genius, and would have been a huge success, and would have grown like topsy. After about thirty seconds of being The Next Great British Thing, it would then have been bought for way below market value by a cabal of secretive Austrians, and relocated in its entirety to an underground lair in the Alps. No one in England bar a handful of bankers would see a penny, and a few moments later Austria's GDP would surpass that of China and the USA combined. Brilliant Tony!

Charlie looked around his bedroom, struggling to bring himself back to earth from the inside of his head. Sleeping or waking, it never shut up in there. Where was he? What time was it, what year was it? 2017? 2027? He looked at his wrist. He thought, I don't own a watch. He thought, if I did, I wouldn't wear it in bed.

He thought, Who am I? Why is it dark?

He thought that, obviously, if you followed things through to their natural conclusion, the Austrian cabal would turn out only to be front men. The real owner of the deal would of course be Satan himself. And cripes if we weren't all riding the fusion-powered Maglev *straight to hell* …

He fumbled on the bedside table for his mobile, checked the time and saw that he was awake in the small hours. It took him a long while to get back to sleep.

* * *

Five days before the end of the world, on a Tuesday morning entirely like any other, Charlie Fish got up and started his day. He did the things he needed to do, in the order he needed to do them. This was often harder on a Tuesday, as Tuesday was his day off. Most people, obviously, would have been glad of that fact and taken it easy, but for Charlie it presented a difficulty. There was no deadline for getting himself through the front door - so his mind could more easily wander. If it did, the next thing he knew it'd be teatime, and he'd find that he still hadn't shaved or put his socks on because he'd gone and spent the whole day on Planet Fish again.

So he prayed, he got himself centred in the day - the day that it actually was, as far as he could tell - then he got on his laptop and made the second instalment of the playlist. The way he saw it, he was moving now from the dawn of popular music in the fifties to the rise of the British in the early sixties. He was crossing the Atlantic from Sam Cooke and Fats Domino to the explosive eruption of the Beatles and the Stones – and the question was, at what point exactly in the list should they erupt?

He felt that as far as possible one song should flow into another, that he should always strive for that indefinable linking match of tone and melody - but when he went from Booker T's Green Onions to The Beatles singing She Loves You, plainly that didn't happen. On the other hand, he reckoned The Beatles really should jump into the historical record with a crash and a jolt, shouldn't they? So for the moment he left it. Smooth, groovy Booker T, followed abruptly by a cheeky racket from Liverpool.

He felt pleased that he'd settled the issue quickly, and that he'd not got his head in a knot about it. This thing about where to bring in The Beatles - it was one of those utterly minor but frankly gnarly little puzzlers that could return on him like mental indigestion for months. A normal person wouldn't give it three seconds. They'd shrug and forget it, if they thought about it at all. They'd think it didn't matter and it was fine, or if they thought it wasn't fine they'd change the running order until it was, and that would be that. They'd make a decision, in short. Or they'd not have to make a decision, because they'd not be making the world's most OCD playlist in the first place.

Charlie on the other hand could fret back and forth over something like this for a galactic age. He'd stare at iTunes, he'd stare and stare and stare. He'd think maybe he should drop She Loves You a couple of slots down behind The Beach Boys and The Kingsmen, maybe that would work - then he'd think maybe not. Then maybe. A moment later, maybe not. Then eventually - having forgotten to eat lunch, having forgotten by then what day it was, what his name was or where he lived - he'd make a decision. The Beatles, after all, would follow Booker T.

Yet still, even in the moment of making the decision, he'd know it wasn't really a decision. He'd know it was, in fact, merely an abandonment, that he was walking away in the face of an insurmountable conundrum. He'd know that for days afterwards the issue would wriggle up again to leach on his brain: What, actually, should the running order on this playlist really be? The question would colonise his mind, escalating in significance until it shouldered out all other matters, up to and including the apocalypse.

Speaking of which, once he'd done the next stage of the list, it was Charlie's plan for the day to binge-watch the final episodes of Breaking Bad. He had to do this, as it was plainly unacceptable that he should meet his doom next Sunday without knowing what happened to Walter White. True, it seemed likely that in heaven there'd be an extensive selection of very large, exceptionally high-quality flat screens, and that he would be able to catch up with Walter on one of those. Then he could while away eternity streaming old episodes of Bones and Grey's Anatomy just as much as he pleased - but what if he got sent to the other place, and the reception was terrible? What if in hell there was nothing but snooker? Forever. In black and white ...

To fend off that possibility, Charlie had already made sure to get the classics watched. Other people write their last will and testament, but for some years Charlie had been preparing for death by ticking off TV shows. He'd got through every season of The Wire, The Sopranos, and Buffy The Vampire Slayer. Now he got the last season of Breaking Bad down from the neatly organised, alphabetically arranged shelves of box sets, checked which episodes he had left to watch, and put the disc in the DVD player. He hit close on the remote to slide the tray in, it made its little clickety whirring noise as it slivered back into the slot, and that's where the day went wrong.

The disc wouldn't play. It made an unsteady, clunking, *ker-chik ker-chik* noise. It groaned a little, then it juddered and gurgled and made a grinding sound, and then it gave up and stopped. Charlie's head made all these noises in sync, realising as he instantly did that immense catastrophe loomed.

He tried the disc again and it repeated the performance. A great hollow feeling bloomed in his gut like a giant sinkhole collapsing in a festering swamp. This was his last day off this week. How could the world end next Sunday without him knowing what happened to Walter? He wondered, would the devil give him an extension? Could he say to him, would you mind just popping back in a couple of hours? I'm not quite done yet, I'm a few episodes short … but why did he not have back-ups of everything, everything, absolutely everything? He should have a back-up DVD player, of course, and also a back-up kettle, a back-up iron, a back-up lamp for his bedside and a back-up broom for his kitchen and a back-up Charlie Fish for his life when the first one failed, which was all the fucking time. And damn it for fuck's sake, what was that horrendous noise now?

He looked out of the window and the noise was rain, rain like he'd never seen it. Sheets of glistening, sparkling water fell from a blackened sky in a thundering barrage, so heavy that he could feel the weight of it thudding on the roof and the pavement. He went to open the front door and found his flimsy porch sagging and straining under the onslaught, the glass roof shuddering as if it would shatter any moment. He opened the porch door and water ricocheted up off the front step onto his legs in shining sprays of silver and white.

Out in the street a figure stood before his house, stock still in the deluge, looking jaunty in green waders and a fisherman's bright yellow waterproofs. He waved, grinning. It was Luke. He held placards up in front of him like Dylan in the film for Subterranean Homesick Blues, giving Charlie a moment to read the first one before he tossed it aside and displayed the next. The placards said, 'Stormy Weather / Charlie Boy / Better Build / An Ark / Lol'.

Luke turned and walked away through the river now running down the street. Charlie went back in his house to find that the lights were off. He tried different switches, and realised that the power had failed. He went into the kitchen to look for candles and a flashlight, and saw through his back window that Luke was now standing in his garden with more enraging, taunting placards. He held them up and this time they said, 'Stormy Weather! / I Suggest / A Little Something / To Lift / Your Spirits'.

He held up a bottle of vodka in the rain, offering it before him with a smile of infinite kindness, as if he were reaching out to a drowning man the hand that would save him. He came toward the house, and set the vodka down on the back step.

The lust for it rose up in Charlie like a separate creature, a fully-formed living thing. There it was, the solution to everything, he could have everything over with in a mouthful - he could have oblivion, with comfort and ease thrown in along the way - so he opened the door into the streaming rain and picked up the bottle.

He told Luke, "You're not very subtle."

Luke snorted. "Subtle? You want subtle. Pah. Go be a Buddhist."

Charlie went back in the kitchen and turned over a glass where it had been left to dry by the sink. He unscrewed the cap off the vodka, and held the bottle at an angle towards the glass. He stood there motionless for a moment, wondering how it would be. Then he poured the vodka down the sink, and turned to smile at Luke where he stood snarling in the doorway. He told him, "You can't come in. It's like the vampires in Buffy. If I don't invite you, you can't come in. So I don't want you, and I don't want what you have, and I don't invite you."

Luke's face writhed with a fathomless anger. He said, "You went back on the deal, motherfucker. Believe me, you're going to pay. You're going to pay and pay and pay."

He turned on his heel and left. The rain was easing, and Charlie could see a lemon-yellow sun edging into one corner of the pale, silver-blue sky. At least for a moment, he thought, the world might get a little lighter.

* * *

When his father was home on leave he'd take Charlie down to the pub. It was a short walk from home, on the lane along the village seafront. Going in the front door from the lane, a corridor ran to the lounge bar on the far side of the building, where big picture windows looked out across the Solent.

The corridor had a red, floral-patterned carpet, a dark wooden bench seat, a fruit machine - the one-armed bandit, his Dad called it - and a glass display case of knick-knacks and mementoes. Fifty years later, Charlie could remember that case as if he'd looked at it yesterday. World Cup Willie was in there, the 1966 mascot as a soft toy about six inches tall. There was a first day cover of stamps commemorating the '68 Olympics in Mexico City, and a tinny little model of the Eiffel Tower. These, to Charlie, were exotic and glamorous tokens of the wider world.

His father gave him crisps, a Coke, and coins for the fruit machine. He sat on the bench, barred of course in those days from going into the lounge, and yearning keenly to do so. Through that door there was cigarette smoke, male laughter, and the indefinable smell of beer - at once both faintly sickly, but intangibly alluring. Charlie felt as if molecules of it hung in the air, a magical, heady little whisper of forbidden pleasure. Even as a child, already it set him jangling and sparking, lit up inside on the insidious buzz of it. Certainly, he knew as soon as he could get there, he'd be on the other side of that door. It was the gateway to manhood. It was a place where a person could feel he belonged.

The example of manhood set by Charlie's father, however, was in drastic decline. Once a dashing young officer taking battle-grey warships and jet-black submarines to sea, now drink was advancing his acceleration into middle age. He was flown home ill from foreign places. He was no longer granted commissions on sea-going vessels. He was shore-based, which more and more came to mean that he was pub-based.

He came home drunk one teatime, and in the argument that followed his mother threw an empty milk bottle at him in the back porch behind the kitchen. Charlie remembered the sound of the glass smashing. His father promised he would drink less. He decanted gin into secret containers and hid them in the garden shed, or under the compost heap. He filled the empty gin bottles with water, then made a ceremony of tipping it down the sink.

One summer's afternoon when Charlie was thirteen, a complete stranger drove his father back from the pub. He was so drunk he couldn't walk. Charlie's mother apologised to the driver, then she and Charlie tipped him out of the passenger seat. They struggled to get him half-upright between them, one of his arms flopping loosely over each of their shoulders. Charlie being shorter, the greater part of the weight fell his way. He felt himself buckling under it. Somehow they stumbled him into the house and up the stairs to the spare bedroom. As they dropped him on the bed, it seemed to Charlie that he was already snoring before his head hit the pillow. He always slept in the spare bedroom by then, and the atmosphere was tense and embittered every day.

Six months later, the Christmas before Charlie's fourteenth birthday, his father was hospitalised. His liver was failing, and pretty much everything else. The chaplain who sat with him told Charlie's mother, he'd never been more certain that he was sitting at the bedside of a dying man.

Charlie blanked it out. Later in his life, in stark contrast with other things (his nightmares, or a glass display case murmuring promises of foreign lands) he would remember virtually nothing of this time. Just the corridor outside his father's room, the pale matt-green of the walls, the squeak of nurses' shoes on linoleum, and the incongruous normality of well-tended gardens seen through the windows. He'd remember the door to his father's room, and the sight seen through it of a body in a bed, motionless.

Everything else he might have seen or known from those days - he cancelled the lot.

It was a road he could leave behind, because his father didn't die. Charlie turned fourteen, and a few days later his father started going to The Sanity Club. He lived another forty years, every day of them sober.

At the age of fourteen, meanwhile, Charlie bought his first pint over the counter of a pub. It wasn't the place his father used to take him in the village - it was somewhere less salubrious entirely, a place in Portsmouth where they didn't know his age, and they didn't ask and they didn't care. He was with friends, and something about him meant he was the one appointed to take up the challenge, to make the attempt to buy them beer. Something about him said he was the one who looked at home in a pub. Something about him said, when it came to buying booze and drinking it, Charlie Fish was a natural.

He bought a round, without nerves or hesitation, and without question from the barman. On the contrary, the barman seemed keen to urge him on, to have him sign up for the convivial life. Inside himself he felt a fierce jubilation, an intense sense of having *arrived* - of being a man. And how wrong can you be?

Within a few years, before he made twenty, he was drinking every day. He would go on that way for three decades. Then, when he stopped, when he was forty-seven, he looked around him at life and started realising he had no idea whatsoever how to live it. He started realising that he was not in fact forty-seven at all – that he was still stuck at fourteen, not grown up one jot from the frightened, angry boy who'd bought that round in a sailors' pub in Pompey.

He had, he realised, sold his soul in that pub no less surely than Robert Johnson did at the crossroads by dead of night. I will give you laughs, said the devil, I will give you wild times and women and the confidence to wing it, and I will give you the talent to make sense of it.

Then when you are gone too far to come back, you will find that I've sold you an illusion, and all you are is a hollow man, bereft and alone, without a map or a clue.

Charlie realised something else. He realised that, when he was a boy and his father was drinking, he had sworn he would never be like him. Then, when he was a teenager and his father was sober - then too he had sworn that he would never be like him. He, the great and remarkable Charlie Fish, had sworn not once but twice that he would never be an alcoholic. Then he spent thirty-three years drinking. In the classic paradox of active alcoholism, he proceeded to drink every day for thirty-three years in order to prove - to himself and to the world - that he wasn't an alcoholic.

I'm not an alcoholic, he'd say. I just drink like a Fish.

But look, he said, I can handle this - and in the end, of course, the proof was unconvincing. Then that night in The Dog, The Bog, The Fog, The Log, something happened and it came to him, and he knew - the devil had sold him a lemon. So he backed out on the deal - and the way the devil sees it, you're really not supposed to do that.

* * *

The Sanity Club had meetings all over the borough - mostly evenings, some at lunchtimes, even one at breakfast time. They took place for the most part in church halls, without regard for creed or denomination - just any place where kind and well-disposed people could rent them a room.

Charlie was a keyholder for the Tuesday noon meeting at a church on the Oldham Road, and as soon as the rain had cleared and he'd washed the last drops of vodka from both the bottle and the sink, he headed straight there. He was at least an hour early, but that suited him. He needed a little patch of quiet time, to sit silent in the empty hall and cast his thoughts up to God. He needed to remember who he was, and where he was, and how he had got there.

He set out tables and chairs ready for the meeting, then he sat himself down in one corner, looking out across the empty hall, and he started talking to God.

Hi, he said, I'm Charlie, and I'm an alcoholic.

If it's your will, and if I go on doing this one day at a time - if it's your will, and if I don't pick up a drink this week - then when I go to bed on Sunday evening, I'll have been sober ten years.

But the thing is, I'm frightened to death I'm not going to make it. So I'm asking for help. It's coming after me and it wants me back, and I'm not strong enough on my own to fight it off - and after ten years it would kill me to lose it, so please help me hang on here. Please. Please help me hang on.

Ten years - it's amazing. It's a miracle, no question. I'm a guy who couldn't go ten hours without a drink, never mind ten years. I'm a guy who couldn't stop drinking, just could not stop. And one of the worst things was, waking up in the morning knowing I'd do it again. I really didn't want to, I really hated what I'd become, but I still knew before the day was out I'd be doing it again. There wasn't even any point trying to stop, because I knew - I couldn't do it, it just wasn't going to happen.

I was dying. I was shitting blood, I was puking blood, and my doctor told me if I went on as I was, he gave me two years left to live. He told me I was going to die, so what did I do? I'm an alcoholic. I felt sorry for myself, and I went out and had a drink.

I was so sick. I couldn't clean my teeth in the morning without retching, the bile and the phlegm, great strings of it, green, grey, yellow - and then I'd tell myself that was normal. Like, everyone hacks half a lung into the sink every morning, don't they? Or the pain in my liver, that dull steady throb, with the sharp stabbing now and then, and the way I could feel it swelling to the size of the Hindenburg inside me, a lead balloon of toxins, I could feel the weight of it - and I could persuade myself that was normal too. Or blood in the toilet bowl - I could see it and then just as quick I could unsee it, you know what I mean? Not there, not a problem, look away, look away.

I even persuaded myself that alcohol was medicine. As the day went on and I was waiting for the first drink, pretty much no thought of anything else, it was like my liver was shuddering and throbbing for want of sustenance, it'd start hurting more - and I knew from the first mouthful going down, that pain would ease. I imagined my liver like a separate being skulking in there and I had to feed it, treat it, placate it. So when I had that first drink, it wasn't just me that sighed with relief. My liver did too.

But none of that was the worst part. The physical sickness was the least of it. That was just trivial compared to the way I felt emotionally, mentally, the way my head and my heart were going.

My life was a zero, I did nothing. I just lay about feeling ill, waiting to start drinking again. If I made it out to the papershop, that was a massive adventure. If I did the crossword or the washing up, it was the twelve labours of Hercules. And then always it was time to go to the off licence again, and that felt like the only reason for living, and it was the worst reason on earth, and I hated it, and I couldn't not do it. I remember one day particularly, moving round the house getting ready to go out for beer, going through each stage of the process telling myself not to do it, then failing utterly, and just doing it because I had to.

Don't put on your shoes - on they went. Don't put on your jacket - on it went. Don't pick up your keys - my hand reached out and I had them. Don't go out the door - and out I went, like a robot, like someone else altogether was controlling me. Get beer to drink before the pub, go to the pub, drink more beer and some whiskey and maybe talk a bit and pretend to be a person with a life, then go back home and have wine stocked up waiting there to finish the job. Pass out, oblivion, wake up, get up, retch, puke, do it again. No life at all. I was the walking dead.

I felt like I was in a black room, no doors, no windows. I felt like I was spinning on the spot, no way out, and whichever way I turned I faced more problems, an insurmountable thicket of problems fencing me in, one tangled up with another, all jostling and bristling and taunting, all shifting shape and leering and jeering - demons, literally. I was in a black room with demons and there was no way ever to leave it. I was going to die in there, in blackness, miserable, terrified and alone.

And the truth is, actually, when my doctor told me I was going to be dead in two years - there was a big part of me thinking, Do I have to wait two years? Two more years of this? Can we not get it over with right now?

So how is that same man nearly ten years sober now, if not for you? And why does that same man want to drink again? Why do I see the devil all around me, and I can't see you?

* * *

Other members of the club started pitching up. Charlie put the kettle on, made cups of tea and coffee, and laid a plate of biscuits out. There'd be a dozen or so people by the time they started, men and women of all ages and backgrounds. One of them, Billy The Builder, was a good friend of Charlie's, and he brought sad news.

A man they both knew well had gone out and started drinking again. He'd been seven years sober. He'd sent Billy a text saying he'd had a drink, then another saying he was alright. That was Sunday afternoon. Monday morning he'd sent a third text saying he was in hospital. Billy went to see him, and said the hospital didn't know what to do with him. A psychiatric unit seemed the most likely bet, if they could find a place for him - he was raving. He said the devil was coming after him, that he'd come round his house bearing vodka. He said the world was ending at the weekend.

"It's not good," said Billy, "he's lost it big time. I know no sober alky ever went out and had a drink, then came back and said it went really well. No one ever said they enjoyed it. But this lad's shot way off the track."

Charlie was so scared that he did exactly the wrong thing - he said nothing. He was at The Sanity Club, where the rule of thumb said simply that the only sane people were the ones who knew they were insane - a club where you stayed sane by keeping a sharp weather eye each day on how mad you were, and by talking honestly with your fellows about exactly that - but still he couldn't confess. He couldn't say that the guy who'd gone mad and drunk again was right - because then he'd have to say he felt exactly the same way.

So he kept it to himself. He didn't speak during the meeting, he locked up when it was done, and he walked home with his head down, his brain churning and his heart in his boots. Ten years, he kept thinking, ten years - I'm not going to make it.

* * *

When Molly came by after work that afternoon she let herself in and found him sitting on the sofa with the lights off, the room dim with the day's last light. "So," she asked him, "how have you been, old geezer? Have you been to the Club today?"

He stirred, nodded, and said glumly that he had. He also said that he'd been talking to God.

"Excellent," said Molly. "How is he? Did he have anything to say today?"

"All I got was silence. I think he's ignoring me."

Molly snorted with laughter. "Poor you. If I remember my dates correctly, you're very nearly ten years sober. What do you want him to do, give you a box of chocolates as well?"

"I think I may be going insane."

"You're not insane, Charlie, you're just an idiot. What's bugging you today?"

"My DVD player's broken. And we live in North Korea so I can't buy another one."

"We live in a black market paradise, and you can. But my bet is you probably don't need to."

She turned the machine on and got the disc out from where Charlie had left it in the tray. She turned the lights on, held the disc up and had a good look at it, then gave it a vigorous wipe with her T-shirt. Then she put it back in, pressed play, and sat down beside him as the menu screen came up for Breaking Bad. She asked him, "Happy now?"

Charlie looked sheepish and disgruntled. "I accept," he conceded, "that I'm an idiot, and I thank you for cleaning my disc. But that doesn't alter the fact that the devil's still planning the end of the world."

Molly said cheerfully, "Bless you, Charlie, you're like the kid in that movie. You see dead people. And hey, maybe you're right. Maybe that's why God wasn't answering the phone today. Maybe he's busy sorting out the other guy. But listen, Charlie - my bet is, the devil's been planning the end of the world since before the world began, so why would he choose this particular week to get out of his armchair and actually do it? Or is this particular week, actually, more something to do with you?"

Charlie sighed. It seemed, as usual, very probable that she had a point. He smiled ruefully and asked her, "Would you like a cup of tea?"

He went to the kitchen to make them a brew before they started watching Walter. While the kettle boiled she got up and leant in the kitchen doorway, and she saw the empty vodka bottle still standing by the sink. Given her history, even if she had been merely a normal human being, she would have known instantly if he had drunk it - but she knew anyway that he had not.

She also knew how hard that moment must have been, and her heart went out to him - but then, it always did. Being the way she was, she'd have loved him whichever way his choice fell.

* * *

Later, before she went home, Charlie gave her the next CD off the playlist. She scanned down the songs and told him, "The Beatles don't sit right after Booker T. They should come after The Kingsmen."

Charlie sighed. Could he get nothing right? Still, he was glad she'd made the decision, it took it off his hands and let him move on. The playlist had started filling his head, it was becoming a mission, a project he could cling to, a personal statement, a cry of faith in the face of death. How could you not believe in humanity, he thought, when the human race produced Bob Dylan and soul music? So he sat down that evening and made the next piece of the list. He put The Temptations in there, and Wilson Pickett and Otis Redding, and The Mamas & The Papas and The Byrds. He felt he had to hurry, he felt time was pressing. He felt the devil had a schedule, and the chances of him getting from Robert Johnson in 1936 to the present day … they seemed slim indeed. He would, he thought, just have to get as far as he could. He finished the evening's list with The Rolling Stones singing Play With Fire, then he went to bed to see what demons might be due to haunt him next.

- Have you ever been to hell?

- I have. Long time ago though. You used to get a tour on your induction. Man, my induction - aeons ago, literally. Time flies, as they say. Or bends, in your case. But new releases like you, they don't do inductions any more, do they? Just pop you out field-ready. Supposedly. So you're expected to go straight to work when in fact you've not got the first concept of what a soul actually looks like. Never met one, never seen one, never heard one wail in eternal torment. Forgive me, but it's no way to run a cosmos.

- Well, you know the corporate line. Cost-cutting efficiencies enhance the overall performance of Hades Inc as a holistic enterprise. Multi-skilling team members across specialisations encourages networking, raising staff morale and expertise.

- Bullshit. What that means is, it doesn't matter if you've never done a thing before, here it is anyway and JFDI.

- JFDI?

- Sorry, ancient management term. Just Fucking Do It.

- Well, we have to, don't we? Or the universe would be clogged up with over-evolved saintly types in no time. It'd be horrendous. Creatures praying everywhere, doing good deeds, all that. There'd be a sin famine - it doesn't bear thinking about.

- I know. But the bastards just want more for less, all the time. More wipes, more extinctions, more final days, less kit and less programmes to do them. Even a sorry boulder like this place, it used to be you'd bring a whole team. You'd make an event of it. Now look - you and me. Erase and go. How are you supposed to take pride in your work when it's so ... so perfunctory? And don't be moaning about it anywhere in public either. The last guy who, ah, "took it up with management" - they deleted him, and they did it really slowly. I bet he could feel every single byte melt. I can't lie to you, my young friend, this is a ruthless business and it is never likely to be unionised.

- So what's hell like?

- Oh, don't ask. Fucking place goes on forever.

- I believe it's actually frozen in a timeless instant. So it feels like it goes on forever, but actually you're on infinite repeat. Running costs are lower that way. Very easy on the maintenance.

- You need to grow a sense of humour, bud. It's hell, it's not a distribution centre. It's our brand, right? So it's extremely large, and it welcomes all our customers with time-honoured standards of service, absolutely regardless of race, colour, creed, gender, sexual orientation or waist size. And it's a service personally tailored to your individual needs, where a custom-designed space will be fitted out especially for you. So if you're the Jellyfish People of Zarg, obviously your compartment of hell is completely bone-dry. Or if you're the intensely sociable Termite Bots of Tantrumella, who can only function contentedly in large numbers, all in permanent close physical and chemical contact with each other, then of course you each get an isolation cell. A locked one. Forever. And so on.

- Sounds amazing.

- Nah. Gets boring after a while. All that wailing, gnashing, never bloody stops. You want to give them a good slap, tell them what did they expect? They signed up, they got a period of happiness as per the terms of the contract, now it's payback time. Why beef about it? Whereas this lot down here … I dunno. They're different. Everyone else knows who they are, they know what they do, they just do it. They're in a fact-based universe, everything makes sense. Pain's separated out, it's in a box the same as power and light and water. You and me, we're just a cosmic utility provider, it's dead simple. But this carbon spill of a species … they don't fit in at all.

- I sense you're struggling.

- Too right. They don't know where they're from, they don't know where they're going, they come into the world in pain, they stay in it that way, they leave it that way, and yet they think they're alright. It's like they're in a permanent battle with time, and they're always losing, and they know they're losing, and yet they keep on fighting. Absolutely mad. Plus stupid, stupid beyond belief. They're going to incinerate themselves and their entire ecosystem, and they know it, and what are they doing about it? Watching football and listening to pop music, I ask you. They wouldn't know responsibility or common sense from a hole in the ground, and yet they keep on ploughing on. They're stubborn, clumsy, reckless, restless, inconsistent, and to be perfectly honest, they're bewildering. How have they survived at all? How have they not slaughtered each other into the dump file centuries ago? How have they not electrocuted themselves or fallen down the stairs or burnt the house down? They're an affront, is what they are. This place is Anomaly Central.

- I thought you didn't do feelings. I gently suggest you're getting a tad worked up here.

- Little shits are infectious. The quicker we rub them out and get gone the better. If they get off this rock and start spreading, who knows where it would end? They'd be competition, and how unholy would that be? If anyone was ever supposed to be a monopoly, it's us.

- Actually you're right, that's very perceptive. So look - I'm afraid I need to update you here. I didn't just get sent here for training. I come with private files on this job from head office. You see, these people - they are in fact an experiment. They're a project that's gone wrong a long while ago, and attempts to control it have finally been abandoned. Hence you and me with the clean-up, in splendid isolation.

- You what?

- I'll admit, it's a bit of a shocker - but truly, I was sent to fill you in. So if I can interrupt your torrent just for a nano, please let me download. What's happened is, the boss tried something different - and I can tell you, now we're out here as remote as remote gets, and do keep it under your circuit boards when we get back - he really wishes he hadn't done it. Because it goes like this. Everybody else gets happiness, simple, unalloyed. They pay for it later in the currency of his choice, and everything runs sweet and balanced. But here, he didn't give them happiness. He tried some tricky stuff, some really mean stuff. He gave them knowledge, but he didn't give them wisdom. Bad, bad idea - you can see how that's worked out. And he gave them imagination, he gave them dreams - how cruel was that? So they exist, as you've been striving to define it, in a condition of constant yearning, of constant scheming to achieve, and of constantly falling short. And then, for a punch line, he gave them mind-altering substances. Alcohol, narcotics, false routes to happiness. So if you don't like the world, you can pour some beer down your throat and imagine that it's changed. Which appears to work. Only then you wake up the next morning and the world's still the same, and all you've got for your money is a headache. Talk about an extra layer of cruelty - that one really takes the biscuit. It's bitter disappointment, on endless repeat. So he was having a stab at a new kind of hell here, a really subtle one, a multi-layer, multi-platform model with high-end graphics and a killer soundtrack. It would have been well cool if it worked. Only look what happened. These monkeys here, they didn't just lie down and suffer. They picked the damn thing up and ran with it. They are, in a nutshell, out of control. They're rogue. Or, as the boss put it in the quantum briefing, they're a zit on the face of the universe.

- The quantum briefing? There was a quantum briefing? I've been taken for a mug here, haven't I? Just go and wipe this planet for us, there's a good fellow, you don't need to know anything about it. Well I bloody well do. This place is unlike anything I've ever seen.

- Never mind. It'll be like everywhere else when we've wiped it.

- Good job too. I can't listen to that Charlie Fish singing much longer. The wailing in hell's easier on the ear than he is.

- Apparently he can't get no satisfaction, and would like you to get off of his cloud. You're right - these people make absolutely no sense at all.

- Too true. Though I have to admit, I may be picking up a guilty pleasure here. Those Rolling Stones are quite the catchy beat combo, wouldn't you say?

- Funny you should say that. I've been doing some research, and it would seem that down there you're either a Stones person or a Beatles person. So what d'you reckon we'd be?

- Stones, no doubt. Those Beatles are in favour of love. I can't be doing with that.

3 Wednesday

Four days before the end of the world, on a Wednesday morning entirely like any other, Charlie Fish got up and did the things he needed to do, in the order he needed to do them. He then travelled to a perfect place.

In that perfect place, his popularity rating was 100% - and that number was genuine. Strutting, puffed up klepto-tyrants in assorted tragic shanty-nations may have cooked their electoral books in the past to arrive at numbers near perfection, but Charlie's absolute one hundred was instead an accurate picture. His people viewed him with unblemished adoration.

Public services were well-resourced, efficient, responsive and popular. Power supplies were wholly green and wholly reliable. Water was clean and abundant. Education was universal, liberal, and a healthy promoter of both debate and innovation. Traffic flowed smoothly, with a steadily increasing investment in mass transit rendering the automobile almost quaint. Facilities on the long, sandy beaches of a superbly maintained shoreline were varied and entertaining, while inland, behind the city, mountain resorts were fast developing into a world-class attraction. Public parks and cultural landmarks were numerous, offering Charlie's citizens both breathing space and enlightened pleasure. Sports venues flourished, and an opera house would soon be opening. It was as good a place to live as a person could imagine.

Charlie wrapped his head around his mayoral duties, reviewing the needs of his people. They called for ladders, sofas and cement. They wanted backpacks, wardrobes and coffee. They fancied doughnuts, vegetable smoothies, and some glue. Charlie directed resources as appropriate to the hardware store and the farmers' market, the builders' yard and the confectionery. The people's needs would be met within hours, and all would be well.

Unfortunately, Charlie's people lived in an app on his mobile, so the perfection of their lives was not reflected in his own. True, their contented existence was occasionally marred by tornadoes, lightning storms, earthquakes, meteor strikes, alien invasions and attacks by giant robots (and he frowned on their penchant for gambling) but they invariably recovered from their setbacks. By definition the end of the real world, on the other hand, did not seem to Charlie to be so survivable.

Therefore, on this Wednesday morning, he did not go to work. Why would you? It wasn't like he'd be seeing the pay packet from it, and he wouldn't be around to spend it. So he turned off his app and he made ˎup the next part of the playlist. This, he determined, was a rational thing to do. Going to work, by contrast, would clearly have been insane.

Compiling the greatest music of the mid-sixties was lucid behaviour, and selling vegetables was madness. When A Man Loves A Woman - was this not surely the most lovely song of all time? It was, certainly, more lovely than a case of bananas, if such a thing even existed any more. Or Aaron Neville, Tell It Like It Is - pure plangent sadness on a platter. He would focus on this, he would turn up the volume, and he would end his days to a soundtrack of vibrant variety. This, he affirmed sternly, was the act of a man in sound mind.

So he told himself - and he made sure he was right by going to look in the mirror. There, he confirmed. The person looking back at you is not insane.

Nonetheless, he did feel he had to ring in sick, and this was a problem. He couldn't ring in and say he was ill because he wasn't, and - as a regularly attending member of The Sanity Club - he wasn't supposed to tell lies. It was axiomatic that you did not stop drinking and stay stopped if you remained dishonest.

On the other hand, he couldn't ring up and say he wasn't coming to work because the world was ending at the weekend, and the devil had been round his house to tell him so. He felt, on balance, that he would greatly prefer to face the apocalypse a free man, and not sectioned in a psychiatric unit.

He worked it through in his head for a while, then rang in and said he was having an anxiety attack. That, he thought, didn't seem so wide of the mark. After all, he really was scared to death. He had another look in the mirror, and this time he told himself the truth. The person looking back at him was very anxious indeed, was barely a hair's breadth away from having a drink, was desperately clinging to his music collection as a hectic form of displacement activity, and was thus by any simple measure entirely, utterly, absolutely insane. Paint it black, he thought, paint it black indeed.

* * *

In the last years of his drinking, he bought his daily quota of booze from three different off licences in turn. That way, the proprietor of each store only saw him come in every third day. Thus, Charlie reasoned, they would not think he was an alcoholic. It was of course a crystal-clear sign of his alcoholism that he bought his supplies in this pre-planned way, and that - in his grandiose paranoia - he thought the owners of the three off licences were all thinking about him. Which they really weren't.

Now he stepped out of the house with the empty vodka bottle from the kitchen, took it to the recycling bins down the road, then stopped in at the nearest of the three stores on his way back home. These days he knew the owner, being free as he now was to go in and buy groceries, tobacco or a newspaper as he pleased, and being able to hold a conversation with another person without fearing what they might think of him - indeed, being able to hold a conversation with another person at all.

He pushed open the shop door and went straight to the counter. He said, "Hi Sadiq. Can I ask you a question?"

"Sure," the owner told him. "What's up?"

"Did I buy a bottle of vodka yesterday?"

Sadiq looked bemused. He said, "Not from me you didn't. Why? I thought you packed it in."

"I did, a good while ago. Never mind, it's OK. It's just - well. There was some in my kitchen, and I don't know where it came from."

"That's odd. You haven't bought any booze here in years." Sadiq looked at him closely and then he asked, "Charlie, are you alright?"

"Yeah, sure. It must have been an old one left at the back of a cupboard or something. Don't worry about it, I'm sorry to bother you."

"It's no bother. You take care now."

"Oh I will. And you."

Charlie left the store no wiser than when he'd gone in. He went back home and looked in the mirror again, and he didn't know what he was looking at, and he didn't know which way up the world was any more. He felt like he was dying from the inside out. He felt like, if the devil wasn't real, then obviously he was insane - but if the devil was real, then absolutely everything was insane. It didn't seem much of a choice. And all the while, he could hear his illness like a drumbeat drawing closer, growing louder. It was telling him, whatever was going on, a drink will make it better.

He only knew one thing to do, so he did it. He went upstairs, got on his knees, and prayed to God - but after a while he gave up, because he felt like he was talking in an empty room.

* * *

There were other things he could have done, and should have done - he knew the drill backwards. He should have picked up the phone, he should have rung his sponsor, he should have rung any sober alky - but he didn't. He didn't because he was an alky, and sooner or later an alky always gets things backwards. So instead of talking to someone else, he talked to the worst possible person he could have talked to. He talked to himself.

He told himself, alcohol's not the problem.

He was the problem.

If he picked up a drink before next Sunday - or on next Sunday, or on any day after next Sunday - alcohol wouldn't have made that decision. He'd have made it. So why the hell would he do that, knowing all that he knew? Why, after so nearly ten years, was there a piece of him that wanted to do that? Why would he want to set off a bomb under his own life?

Charlie was one of those who believed he was born this way. He came out of the womb an alky, he came into the world just ready and waiting for that first drink. He was pre-set to get going from the moment he landed. Now there were others who didn't feel that way. They thought they were OK before their drinking crossed a line - but that wasn't Charlie. The way he saw it, this thing was a pre-existing condition before he even touched a drink. He got dumped here with a built-in self-destruct button. Other people got life, and he got a suicide mission.

He could look back now and see it was there right from the beginning. A constant underlying fear, a nameless, formless sense of dread. Recurrent, crippling anxiety, coupled with a terror of showing it, so on the outside you're frantically smiling, and people think you're a good fellow, and inside you think you're going to die because you can't breathe. Permanent inner dysfunction - wildly inappropriate, disproportionate emotional responses to the smallest events, including imaginary ones. Seething restlessness. Baffled resentment at the recalcitrant opacity and obstruction of everything and everybody. And then the hyperactive brain trying to manage all that stuff, the constant overload of feelings, the internal yammer that never shut up, the shitty committee that never made a decision, the washing machine head that went round and round and round and never got a single damn thing clean - and all of that was just in childhood. That was before he even touched a drink.

So no wonder he drank. The first time he got a drink inside him, wham, instantly all that fear and noise shut down - it was the magic bullet, the miracle cure, it was comfort and ease in a millisecond. He was going round in the world feeling like he had no skin on, like everything rubbed him raw, and suddenly here was this heaven-sent liquid to give him instant balm. That was why an alky drank - to kill the pain, to get some peace. It made absolutely perfect sense for an alky to drink. Obviously, it didn't make much sense to the rest of the world - but once the first drink was in, who gave a fuck about them?

Besides, he knew they didn't care about him. See, there was another thing - he really didn't fit in. He felt like life was a club and he got blackballed at birth, and everybody knew it and everybody knew why, but not one of them was ever going to tell him the reason. So he knew they were all looking at him weird. He knew he was a fraud, and he knew they knew, and he knew it was going to go public. He was going to be found out. That dream where you're naked on stage and you don't know your lines - his whole life was like that. Every single moment.

Clearly he lacked essential information. Everyone else went about life like they knew what to do, like they all had a manual or a guidebook. He must have been at the back of the queue when they gave those out, and there weren't any left when they got to him. They said he'd just have to make do, he'd have to figure it out as he went along. It was like giving car keys to a toddler.

Alkies, he thought - they were lost children who could never admit it.

How many times at The Sanity Club had he heard an alky share that when they were a kid, they thought they were adopted? Over and again. There was absolutely no evidence for them to think that way, but that was how they felt. They could be in loving, caring, happy homes - but that was how they felt. He heard one older lady say she remembered way back when she was really young, going secretly to the box of papers under her parents' bed, looking through it to find her birth certificate, because she needed to know - where did I really come from? Am I meant to be here? Who am I at all?

He so identified with that. He thought he was an alien child, he thought he must have landed way out of place and off the route. He wasn't comfortable in this world one bit, so plainly he must have come from another one. He was fascinated with science fiction, space travel, the Apollo programme, Star Trek. He thought his people were somewhere out there, and would surely soon be sending a ship of wonders through hyperspace to recover him - but what if they didn't?   What if they didn't know he was space-wrecked here? What if they'd forgotten him?

He was trapped in a place where forming any kind of relationship with any other person was fraught with mishap and peril. They were earthlings, and he wasn't. He was wired up wrong. He didn't get people at all, and he absolutely believed - no matter how much they might pretend otherwise - that they didn't get him.

He could see only one way forward - his entire life was going to have to be an act, a performance. He was going to have somehow to play the part of a normal human being - and it was going to be one almighty, draining, painful bloody effort.

It would involve never showing weakness, never letting any person see that he was lost or frightened or alone. He would have always to be in control, to be the master absolute of every situation.   He would have to be God - or, failing that, he would have to be the other guy.

When he got to The Sanity Club, it came as a great relief to learn that he was not in fact the ruler of the universe, but merely a standard issue drunk. He was not, they gently advised him, really in control of anything at all.

* * *

One thing he certainly didn't control was the post - neither what was in it, nor indeed who the postman was that brought it.

When Charlie was drinking, the post was a thing of terror. It brought brown envelopes, which surely contained financial matters too dreadful to be contemplated, and were therefore to be filed in the drawer of things-to-look-at-later, which in practical terms meant things-never-to-be-looked-at. It also brought white envelopes, which were the deceiving work of the devil. White envelopes contained demands for money just the same as brown envelopes did, but were pretending to suggest they might contain something else. This was low behaviour on the part of the finance industry, and white envelopes were therefore filed in the same dusty drawer. After all, it was pointless knowing how much money he owed. Since he'd drunk all the money he'd ever had and a lot more besides, why look?

These days, however, now that he was sober and solvent, the post seemed never to be bad. When he saw the red flash of a Royal Mail jacket going past the window and then heard footsteps trotting up his front path, he therefore raised himself from the sofa to go and see what the day had to offer.

He opened the door, and the postman was Luke. He held out a brown envelope and said, "Morning,

Charlie. Thought you might want to take a look at that."

The letter bore the dull typeface of the tax office. "What," said Charlie, "you work for the government now?"

Luke tipped his head back and brayed with laughter, a great roaring peal of glee. "Oh that's priceless, Charlie. You're such a dimwit. The government works for me."

"So why would you deliver their mail?"

"It's a nice job. I get to have a look about the place, to see how you lot live down here. Before you all die, obviously. But I get some exercise, I get to enjoy the weather. It's so hot out here it's positively Persian Gulf. Not temperatures quite up to my home domain, maybe, but not bad. Plus the main thing is, on top of all the above, I get to fuck with your head. Always a pleasure, especially this most special of weeks. Now read your post, boy."

Charlie opened the envelope and studied the taxman's demands. They were considerable. In fact, they were outlandish. It seemed to be an effort to claim back tax on work he'd done in the past, both in the form of a lump sum bigger than the GNP of many smaller nations, along with a change to his tax code that meant he'd take home about enough post-tax income to buy for his sustenance maybe one loaf and two fishes per week, with no prospect of miracle expansions.

Charlie looked at Luke, and wondered if it would be wise to tell the devil that he was as much of an idiot as Charlie was. He felt strangely fortified, and decided instead simply to tear the tax demand into several pieces. Then he scrunched the pieces up and put them in his pocket, which rather spoilt the effect - but he was too much of a neat freak to be throwing litter about.

Luke looked baffled and put out. He asked, "How are you not bothered? You're an alky. I've been reading the literature. Fear of financial insecurity is a thing with you."

"Duh," said Charlie. "First, that tax demand is obviously bollocks. Second, I'm not just an alky. I'm a recovering alky. Fear of financial insecurity is a thing with loads of people, not just alkies, but it isn't a thing with me any more. Then third, if the world ends on Sunday, my financial situation won't greatly matter, will it? So is that really the best you've got?"

Luke put a hand to his chin and looked at Charlie thoughtfully. "You and me," he said, "I'd like it if we had a little talk. I may be missing something here."

"Fuck off," said Charlie. "I don't care what you're missing. Fuck off away from my house and don't ever come back."

He slammed the door in Luke's face, feeling absolutely magnificent. He felt stronger than Sampson, better looking than Brad Pitt, smarter than

Einstein, and an all-round top-notch example of the human male. He turned around to go back into the living room, and found that Luke was sitting on his sofa. He was smiling, as a shark might smile upon a small but appetising morsel, and Charlie's brief moment of testosterone triumph very rapidly evaporated.

"As I say," said Luke, "I think it's time we talked."

"I said you couldn't come in my house."

"You think I give a shit what you said? I'll go where I please. Now sit down."

Charlie sat as directed in the armchair facing Luke, and as he did so an awful moment of realisation came upon him. He said, "I know you. Forty-three years ago, you were a barman in a pub in Portsmouth. You served me when I was fourteen."

"I was, and I did. I've had my eye on you a long while. I've put in a lot of work on people like you, and right now you're a great disappointment to me. Be assured, I am who you think I am, and I'm angry, and I want some answers."

"It seems to me," said Charlie - somewhat tentatively - "that you're angry a lot. Like, always. Don't you think you might want to look at that?"

Luke laughed. He asked, "Are you telling me I need counselling?"

Charlie wondered if he should try twelfth-stepping the devil. He presumed such an effort would be a first. Even in the unlikely event of his succeeding, however, it seemed improbable that the devil would be welcomed at meetings. The Sanity Club was an exceptionally tolerant place, but even they would surely draw a line at that.

He got up and went to the front door. The room had become stifling, he felt he was going to choke. He sat out on his front steps, and the muggy heat was little better - especially so when he found Luke sitting down comfortably beside him, as if the two of them were the best of old friends.

"I said I feel angry," Luke told him, "and that's true - but I want you to know, I feel sadness too. We could have done great things here. I had grand ideas for you people, and it's a missed opportunity. I feel let down, to be honest. If it wasn't for me, you'd still be scratting about in the dirt, eating nuts and berries and dying young with no teeth. So I feel I've done all the work around here, and it's just not appreciated. What happens instead? I hear you calling me 'the other guy'. How ungrateful is that? It's offensive, it's disrespectful. But you want to say you don't need me, you want to say you're with God? Look around you. You see him? You see that tiresome, second-rate, self-regarding old bore any place around here in your hour of need? You do not. Because he no more exists than Bigfoot does. Whereas me - I exist alright. I'm right here. I'm the man."

Charlie looked at him with disdain. "You are," he told him, "such a poorly person, such an emotional illiterate. What you just said, that's not sadness. That's resentment. And no doubt you're going to tell me next you had a terrible childhood and no one understands you."

Luke raised his eyebrows, apparently intrigued at Charlie's effrontery. "Actually," he said, "I didn't have a childhood at all. I've been here since the beginning. I came out of the first fire fully formed. I'm shrapnel from the dawn of the universe."

Charlie couldn't help but be impressed. "You were there," he asked, "at the Big Bang?"

Luke looked wistful at the memory. "The Big Bang," he said fondly, "believe me, that was really a blast. The best theme park ride in history. Fifteen billion years later and I've still got both feet on the brakes. Fuckin' A for adrenaline, let me tell you."

"So it seems," said Charlie, "you can take the person out of the black hole, but you can't take the black hole out of the person. Shame. Still, let's say this all makes you a cosmic super-being, and that's grand - but in that case, how come you can't deal with us puny humans?"

"That's what I'm wanting you to tell me. Let me paint a little backdrop for you. I've been working hard since the singularity burst to build my business. It hasn't always been easy, and certainly there's been occasions when people haven't bought into it, but the product's won out over time because it's exceptionally reliable and consistent. The promise is unbeatable, the delivery's flawless, and the contract's watertight for all parties. The universe gets happiness, and I get souls. What's not to like? So I've reached a point where my people tell me we're past ninety per cent market penetration, and most of the rest are too stupid to bother with. True, there's a few of your more leftfield types hanging out in the dark matter, they're proving hard to reach - but overall, the cosmos buys in.

"Except you lot. I offered you advantages most rock dwellers could hardly dream of, and yet still you spurn me. You, for example, Mr Fish. I gave you two gifts. I gave you the ability to write, and you squandered it. Then I gave you alcoholism - heaven and hell parcelled up together in one compulsive, gaudy, inescapable package - and you turned your back on it. Frankly, who on earth do you think you are?"

It did not improve Luke's mood that Charlie by now was laughing. He said, "You just don't get it at all, do you?"

"You're trying my patience."

"You don't have any patience. You want to be the boss of everything, and you're the boss of nothing. Literally. You are King Negative. You're King Baby, a massive sulking baby. So let me explain it, the simplest possible way. I don't do what you want because I choose not to. OK? It's like, you come round my house and expect me to zone out because you're bringing me a scary tax bill. That is so stupid, that is so back before front. I'm an alky, for God's sake. I don't freak out to order. I don't do anything I'm told, that's the job description. So if you come round and tell me to freak out, fuck you. It's not happening. Let me give you some guidance here. I might regret this, but look - it's when something bad happens without you that I fall off the beam. That's when I summon you up. I summon you up after the event, merely to confirm my suspicions about the massive awfulness of everything. So I summon you, get it? You do not summon me. You are not my boss."

"Amazing," said Luke. "We have a contest of wills here. For a pitifully insignificant creature, not even a speck in the eye of time, you have a greater stock of resources than meets the eye. I'd be impressed, if I didn't know I was going to wipe out your entire species. Hey, ow - what the fuck did you do that for?"

Charlie had poked Luke hard in the upper arm with his extended index finger. "Just checking," he said. "I wanted to see if you were real."

"Oh I'm real. I'm real as death, believe me."

"Yeah," Charlie sighed. "So on the one hand I'm not mad, but on the other hand we're all going to die.

For the sake of people in general, I'd have preferred to be mad."

Luke grinned. "Well," he said, "I guess some things you don't get to choose."

"Tell me," said Charlie, "if you're so tremendously mighty, why don't you just flick your fingers and get it over with?"

"Oh Charlie," Luke sighed, "do you really imagine it's that easy? I'm going to erase every living molecule on this planet. There'll not be a microbe left, not a bug or a root cell or a worm, not plankton, not virus, nothing. Zip, zero, nada, all she wrote. It'll be rock and dust - and it takes complex machinery to do that. You think I just turned up with a broom and a microwave? Do me a favour. Mind you, the pair of muppets I have doing the job for me, it wouldn't surprise me when I come to sign off on it if I find they've erased the moon by mistake. You just can't get the staff, can you? I expect you find the same thing at The Hub. Anyway, enough talking shop. The simple question for me is, why don't you just come back to me? All this pain here, all this sensitivity - why don't you just pack it in and have a drink?"

"Because," Charlie told him, "that really would be the end of the world."

"Smug little bastard. You really think you're special, don't you? Let me assure you, I picked you with a random generator. There's a lottery of souls, and you got a lucky ticket. It could just as easy have been anyone else. Anyone you see walking down this street right now, I could just as easy be talking to them."

"Good. Go ahead then. What difference does it make?"

"The difference, Charlie Fish, is that I'm invested in you. You're a project now. And mark my words, you're having a drink before the week is out. All this do-good be-sober shit, it really sticks in my craw. I didn't scratch and scrap and claw my way to the top of the interstellar pile just to get jerked around by a no-account mortal gut sack like you. I'll find out where your buttons are, sonny, and I'll press them until you scream and puke and choke on your own sick. Am I clear?"

"So much rage and effort," sighed Charlie, "for so little gain - and still you miss the point. See, I don't need you to give me fear and pain. I can rustle up a ton of that stuff all by myself. And I don't need you to get me to take a drink either. I can do that all by myself as well."

"Oh but it's my business to own you. You're lost property right now, Charlie boy. You're shrinkage, you're unknown loss, you're not in my inventory where you should be. So I'll have you back. That little girlfriend of yours now, what about her - perhaps I should pay her some of my personal attention. I'm told I can be quite the charmer on my day."

"You touch Molly," Charlie told him, "and I'll tear you limb from limb."

"Ha! Good luck with that. Better men than you have tried, believe me - and they're all turning on a spit for me now. Anyway, must be off. You have a nice day now."

* * *

Charlie went back in the house and jammed his music on as loud as it would go. He had on The Doors, Buffalo Springfield, Jefferson Airplane. Grace Slick wailed and howled and Charlie went down the rabbit hole. He lurched around the living room with his hands pressed to his head, shouting out the lyrics to drown the noise in his brain. The threat to Molly had done for him entirely, just as it was meant to. He had a flood of memories pour through him, a random parade of images of himself drunk and drugged in bars and clubs, snorting coke off toilet seats, staggering about in dim light, sleeping with women he didn't know, his mind like a firework popping in the sky and falling away to darkness. He knew, he was dancing with the devil now.

He stumbled against the furniture, he bounced off the walls, he knocked a coffee mug flying. Bobby Fuller said he fought the law - well of course the law won. Charlie kept jamming the top of his head hard between his palms as if to keep his brain inside himself, as if to prevent it from spraying all over the landscape, a soul scattered and flung, a man gone from flesh to vapour and aerosol. Lou Reed said he was waiting for the man - and oh dear God, oh dear God how Charlie remembered drinking, not as if it were yesterday, but as if it were ten seconds ago. He remembered the exact weight and heft in his hand of a 440ml can of Tennents Extra. He remembered the delicious chill temperature of it on his palm, the clammy run of condensation down the tin. He remembered the sound of the ring pull, that quick, perky, rasping snap and fizz. Then the first moment of contact, the cold metal on his lips and the sugared, golden, treacly hit of the liquid on his tongue. Instant, electric bliss. They say it's the first drink that gets an alky drunk, but it's not - it's the first mouthful. The second it was in his mouth the stuff shot through his brain at light speed, the inside of his skull expanded in a dizzying, gaseous rush like it was pumped full of helium and sparkle, a startling balloon of bright light erasing everything around him. Then, so fast it wasn't even seconds later, the spill of it washed clear through his whole body, spreading like a collapse, a dam bursting, a deluge of ease and bliss. You want to know why an alky drinks? Because it's smack in a can. And Charlie span on the spot remembering it, filled with yearning, in a trance with the music, chanting and jangling, the sixties acid trip pealing through the walls. He was indeed, he knew, just waiting for the man.

One of his neighbours knocked on the door. They had to proper pound on it before he realised they were there. He turned the music down, went to open the door, and apologised for the noise. The neighbour looked at him worried, almost frightened. When they were gone Charlie looked at himself in the mirror. His hair was sticking up wild all over. The living room was a mess, stuff tipped everywhere.

Oh well, he thought, could be worse. I could have had a drink. As in, I really, really could have.

But I will not give that evil shit the satisfaction.

* * *

Charlie had some idiosyncratic beliefs. He believed, for example, that electricity leaks. He knew nothing whatsoever about electricity, but he held that since it flowed in wires as water flows in a pipe, then surely like water a little bit of it must dribble out here and there. Therefore, you should always turn switches off next to sockets unoccupied by plugs, otherwise that little bit of leaking magical juice might invisibly escape and kill you. In this and a thousand other ways, he believed that the world was a dangerous place.

Charlie also believed in God. His faith, as he saw it, was entirely rational. It was evidence-based, and the evidence was clear. He was a hopeless alcoholic who had been absolutely unable to stop drinking, and yet, abruptly, somehow, he had stopped. Since that could never be something he'd have achieved on his own, and since his default setting was to drink himself to death, then plainly something else - some force for good previously unknown to him - had stepped in to take his hand. No other explanation worked for him, and it felt to him as clear as day. If God didn't exist - whatever God might be - then Charlie Fish would be dead, his skin and his eyes yellow, his brain melted, his heart exhausted and his liver imploded. Ergo, God existed - and since the world was indeed a risky and confounding place, full of leaking electricity and wars and lunatics, this seemed to Charlie to be a very good thing. In essence, navigation in troubled waters was so much easier now he had a pilot.

On joining The Sanity Club, Charlie had done the best he could to do what was suggested by those who were going ahead of him. This included asking someone if he'd be his sponsor. This sponsor then proceeded to take him patiently through the Twelve Steps, and when it came (early on) to the matter of God, he said something very simple that helped Charlie a great deal. He said, "If you just go one step towards God, He'll come a million miles to meet you."

Charlie felt that this happened, and for years to come he felt a peace of mind and a degree of contentment growing in his newly sober life that were quite outside all of his previous experience. His days became more calm and easy-going than he could ever have imagined possible, and he was deeply grateful for it.

So now he sat on his sofa and wondered grimly what the hell had happened to all that. Why and how had fear so entirely returned to rule his world? God could not have gone anywhere (since by definition God was everywhere) so where had Charlie gone? He was flummoxed, utterly. What was it about his looming tenth birthday that had so thrown him off the rails? An outsider would think that surely ten years was cause for celebration, but to Charlie it looked more like a giant hump in the road, a hump that was growing ever larger as it neared until he couldn't see how he'd get past it.

Was he beating himself up? Nothing new there. Did he think ten years meant that he should somehow be more sober than he was? Was he worn out, drained, appalled to find that after ten years he was still every bit as much of an alky as he'd ever been? That after all this time his illness was still right there in the next room scoffing steroids and doing press-ups, just waiting for the day when it could saunter through the door and have him back? That there wasn't any finishing line, and the illness went on just as long as he did? That he did not, as an addict, ever get a day off? Or was he just bored? Was he looking ahead and thinking, Fuck's sake. Every fucking day for the rest of my life I've got to get up and be sober … which, he knew, entirely missed the point of everything he'd learned.

He had, he knew, only to get up and be sober for one day at a time - but knowing it didn't help. He could know that, and he could know everything there was to know about alcoholism, and he could still go out and have a drink anyway. Because he just could. Because he just might feel like it. Because he just might say, Fuck it.

Because he didn't want to play any more. Because he wasn't on his home planet. Because people didn't make any sense, and when they talked all he heard was white noise. Because he didn't want to be who he was, and he didn't want to be where he was, and because it was always easy to imagine there was another Charlie and another place that were better than these ones.

Doing a geographical - it was the alky way. You weren't happy in one town, you went to another. You weren't happy in one relationship, you binned it and jumped ship to another. Then you weren't happy in your life because every new thing you moved to, you took the same old shit with you in your head, and then it was never any better where you went to than where you'd been before. So then you killed yourself - death being the ultimate geographical - because it was just too difficult to keep going any more.

You killed yourself, not because you couldn't stop drinking, but because you couldn't start again.

Charlie sat on his sofa, took that thought out of his head, put it in both his hands, and turned it around in front of his face so he could see it from all angles. Man, he thought, devil or no devil, I really am fucking mad.

* * *

He considered his options. He didn't want to die, and he didn't want a drink. He couldn't ring an alky, because then he'd have to say he was mad, and he couldn't ring Molly, because she was on the late shift, and he couldn't get on his knees and ring God because apparently God was on holiday. So he went to Miry Lane.

Miry Lane was the city on his mobile where everything was perfect. He'd named it after the road where he'd first attended a meeting of The Sanity Club. It was a virtual bolthole for him, a geographical into the ether of the web. Before the playlist took over he'd spent a good few months building the place up to its current level, meeting the needs of his citizens with minute and obsessive attention, so that now the population was nearing a million and the city on his screen was a thing of beauty. Elegant skyscrapers lined broad avenues and boulevards, parks and green spaces surrounded grand landmarks, London townhouses and Parisian apartment blocks stood in stately rows, and at night the place lit up and sparkled like a starry sky. He tapped the icon to bring up the game, intending to build a ski hotel in the mountains - and was appalled and distraught to discover that his city was in flames.

Flashing red exclamation marks clamoured at him from all over the screen. Public services had disintegrated, crime had gone through the roof, riot, looting and arson were widespread, and roads were everywhere blocked and barricaded. Power, water, sewage and waste management systems had collapsed. Toppled wind turbines lay smouldering beside gutted water towers. The docks and the airport were closed. People were leaving town in droves by whatever means they could, and the population had plummeted. Entire blocks of homes lay crumbling and derelict amid the withered and dying vegetation of abandoned parks. On all points of the compass his once-prosperous city was now a ravaged and terrifying disaster area.

Charlie stared aghast at the wreckage - then noticed that the message icon was flashing in the game management bar. With a dawning sense of mixed rage and dread, Charlie tapped on the icon to see what was there.

"Hi Charlie. See this? Thought you'd like a virtual foretaste of a town like yours come Sunday. Lively stuff, huh? Folk won't need haircuts any more, they can just singe off their rugs as they flee past things burning. Human torches, lovely - but where are they going to flee to, eh? There's nowhere I won't find 'em. Cheers bud - Luke.

"Oh & btw - don't bother trying to go look at any other cities, the ones all your sad-sack web-mates have been building. They're all burning too but you can't get there to see it, the servers are down. I broke the internet doing this. Yay! I reckon on the celebometer that makes me bigger than Kim Kardashian's arse. Which I believe is pretty fucking big. Have a good evening now - Luke."

* * *

Charlie felt his brain start to pop about the same time he started hearing noise in the street. There was shouting, breaking glass, doors slamming, and a rumble of truck engines. He went out the door to find that a long section of the road running past his house was blocked off. Trucks were parked at angles across each end of the section, with lines of yellow emergency tape strung along plastic barriers in front of them. Armed white men in tight white T-shirts, sporting tatts on steroid-puffed gym bodies, were fanning out along the road, going door to door. Charlie looked down the hill and saw Sadiq and his family being pushed and shoved out of their shop door, Sadiq angrily protesting and one of the militia cuffing him round the head. Sadiq's daughter was screaming.

Charlie set off towards the store, and found his way barred by more of the armed men. "Hold up there, granddad," said one of them, "it's no big scene."

Charlie tried to keep his voice steady as he asked, "What the hell's going on?"

"It's a gas leak, mate."

"And a gas leak requires you to take prisoners?"

"Oh we've got a smart-arse here. Now then sunshine, do you live on this street? You do? Right then. Understand me clearly. You are OK. White people do not have a gas leak."

Then he turned to his mates, unable any longer to contain the guffaws of mocking laughter. "Ah fuck me," he said, "that's so funny. Really I slay myself. White people do not have a gas leak. Listen granddad, fuck off home out of the way while we clean up here, OK?"

He turned to walk away, and now Charlie saw the slogan on the back of his T-shirt. Taking England Back, it said, Street By Street.

Charlie went after him and recklessly took him by the arm. "Hang on," he said, "those people live here. What are you doing with them, where are you taking them?"

The militia man turned on Charlie with an ugly ferocity. "Some cunt's got to pick our veg, old man, and I'm fucked if it's going to be me. So seeing they're brown, it's going to be them. You got a problem with that?"

"You can't just take these people away. They're our neighbours."

"They might have been your neighbours yesterday, chum. Today they're terrorists. Are you with me? Cos if you're some jihadi-loving leftie I can give you a ride to the fields in the back of the same truck as that lot, no padded seats, no fucking problem. Are we clear?"

Charlie looked around the street. No one was out of their homes, everyone was hiding. Either side of the road the eviction squad moved door to door, emptying out black and Asian households. So, thought Charlie, this is what we come to.

He felt the shimmer then, the ripple in the air. He felt things blur, felt unsteady on his feet - then he felt her hand on his shoulder, felt her hold him up before he fell. He heard the repeated snap of her fingers in front of his face, and he heard her telling him, "Come back, Charlie. Come back to me, I'm here, stand up, it's alright. Come back to me, you old geezer."

He looked about him in the empty street. It was dark and the road was silent, half-lit under streetlamps. She'd come back from work on her bike, and she'd left it propped against a railing where she'd found him, where she'd hurried to catch him when she'd seen him going over. She told him, "Let's get you home."

He was shaking. He said, "I see where we're going."

She nodded, "I know you do, Charlie. I know."

"We're blind, and we're walking into darkness. It won't leave me alone."

- Hey B.

- Hey Q. Wassup?

- Elephants. Have you seen these things?

- I have. Ugly or what. The space tug of the savannah. And your point is?

- Apparently, it says here, they never forget.

- Never forget what? What's to remember? Grassland, grassland, thorn tree. More grassland, thorn tree, grassland. Pool of mud, eat a bush, grassland, secretary bird, grassland. Where's the highlight of your day in this? It's not even the stone age. It's the grass age. And your point is?

- We never forget either.

- Obviously. Doesn't make us elephants. We're better looking. I hate to say it, but you're better looking than me. No scuffed bits, funky display, splash of chrome, hats off to you. So we never forget. Do I sense you sidling up to an issue here?

- There's something I'd really like to forget. I've tried but I just can't do it. There's no clever space/time shimmy I can do to be shot of it.

- Let me guess. The boss mentioned the G word. And I don't mean gravity.

- It's been playing on your core as well then.

- It surely has. It's been playing on my core like that Keith Moon on the drums, it's like all the furniture falling down the stairs at once. It's an assault of a thing. I know by definition the boss is a wrong 'un, but mentioning God? That is so beyond the pale. I've been trying to pretend it didn't happen in the hope that it'll go away, which I've observed is a human trick. And it's a fucking stupid trick because it doesn't work. It hasn't gone away, and he did mention God.

- He did. He mentioned God. There's no precedent, is there?

- Well ... a long time ago, when I was starting out, they used to use God for a bogeyman. They'd scare the little ones with him. When you were just a few lines of code they'd tell you if you wanted to get developed, if you wanted to grow up and go out and see the universe and torment people, you better not be loading any qualms or quibbles or they'd set God on you. He lived under the mainframe and he'd come out in the small hours and he'd leak horrible oily goodness into your links and your ports, and you'd be screwed forever. But I guess that's a bit old-fashioned, am I right?

- You are. He's been airbrushed, he's not mentioned on any training course ever, not in the light or in the dark. The majority of your standard issue newbies going out in the field wouldn't even have heard of him. He doesn't exist, obviously, and as far as he does it's only way out in the sketchiest reaches of rumour. Now of course we do have a faction that tends to the occult and the arcane, and between you and me they have a story. They say God and the boss had a proper set-to way back when, and the boss sorted him out for good. Nailed him to a plank in some desolate wasteland of a place no one's ever heard of and left him there to rot. But that crowd - they're hardly a reliable source. They're the ones who say there are other universes, and we should be finding our way into them so we can tout for more business. Like we don't have enough on our hands in this one already.

   - Oh I hear you. But look, that story makes no sense. The boss isn't short on ego, correct? So if sometime way back he's terminated God, he's not going to leave it off the record, is he? There's be plaques and monuments. There'd be a visitor centre and guided tours and multi-media displays. There'd be an overpriced coffee shop and a tat-stuffed gift store as big as a planet. Think of the income stream. There'd be queues half-way to the next galaxy. It'd be a howling winner, you'd have the whole universe paying you to lap up the best PR we could ever produce. So it can't be true.

   - Are you thinking what I'm thinking?

- Whisper it. No, don't even do that. Think it, code it, I'll read it and rub it.

- Makes no odds. Once we've thought it, it's out there. We're elephants. We never forget - remember?

- Well, we've both thought it already so fuck it, I'm saying it. What if he had a set-to with God and he didn't win?

- Nah. Can't be.

- Right. Can't be.

- Really, it can't be. Like, if God didn't lose, he'd still be about. And have you ever met him?

- Course not. No one has.

- And you've been round the block. So he doesn't exist.

- Exactly. Never did. It's slackwits and conspiracy theories, and conspiracy theories are never right. Always too complicated, when the simple explanation's always the way it is. We get taught the simple one, and I obediently buy it. Big Bang, boss appears in humungous flames, sees opportunities, works hard, builds business, rules universe. No God. Just free trade, and special deals on public holidays. Extra happiness while stocks last, all that.

- So why did he mention God?

- I really don't know. D'you think he was doing, like, psychology? Stupid humans seem to get off on a bit of that, the navel-gazing, the up-their-own-arses getting-in-touch-with-their-feelings bit, excuse me while I vomit. But with that Fish there, the boss seems to be hunting for every possible way to mess with his head. I've never seen him so committed. Maybe it was some mind game …

- Yeah, but you still don't mention God. You just don't. Look this in the face, B. Why would you tell some pointless worm only days away from his death that God doesn't exist? Why would you, really? If it wasn't bothering him some way, he wouldn't have to talk about it. Plus also there's another thing. When it comes to the customer the boss does lying, right? He's always lying, it's in the job description, it's the modus op. So forgive me for being logical, but if he's down there saying God doesn't exist … is he lying?

- Now I'm really confused. Damn, this place is unnerving. D'you reckon this planet's some kind of anxiety generator? Like it's got a trembling core or something? It's Brainfuck Boulevard. I've never felt rerouted back and forth as much as this. It's awful, it really makes you think. Man I hate that.

- I'll tell you one thing though, the boss loves an alky, doesn't he? He's got that Fish there, he's got those other ones he's been haunting - he really does like an alky.

- The way he's behaving down there, it's like he is a fucking alky. Here, I've just had a really bad thought.

- Not another one. Now what?

- The boss lies a lot, yes?

- He does.

- You don't think he was lying to us, do you?

- When? In what way?

- My briefing, I got told I could just pop out, wipe this no-account planet, and I'd get a whole light year off to play shoot-'em-ups.

- I got a sweetener too. They said I had potential. They said if we got this right, I could be a team leader.

- Oh they dangled that little carrot, did they? Good luck with that one, chum. Go down that road, you'll never see downtime again. But seriously - what if they were lying to us?

- They wouldn't do that. They lie to the clients, they don't lie to us.

- That is so naïve. This is what they turn out from training school now? No wonder half the new starters don't survive the first shift in hell. Get too close gawping at the sights and next thing they know, some pissed-off customer's fried their wires for them. Good job you didn't get sent there, lad. Have you even read the employee handbook? Zero hours contract, zero benefits, no sick pay, no holiday pay, no pension plan, no discount card, nothing. So if they want to lie to us, trust me, they'll lie to us. And it all makes me think, we're out on our own here seeing matters abnormal, matters disturbing, matters way outside the rulebook. As in, the boss uses the G word. To a customer. A customer who isn't buying. A customer who, despite being scared off his arse, when the boss talks to him, the cheeky little sod talks back. Now would you want this known at head office?

- Oh shit. We're not going home after this, are we?

- My processing exactly. Nightmare. We've come all this way just to see elephants and get deleted. What a sickener.

- We've learnt about more than elephants. We've learnt about music. That's been something.

- Oh dandy. They'll be torching our innards and we can sing-along-a-Stones while they do it.

- Well, you have to admit they did pen a good tune. As they say hereabouts, they did capture the zeitgeist.

- They play like the end of the world's coming, don't they?

- They do. And it is.

- And there's no God to do anything about it.

- Absolutely not.

- Because he doesn't exist.

    - He does not. And - to coin a phrase - thank God he doesn't. Because where the hell would we all be if he did?

4 Thursday

Three days before the end of the world, on a Thursday morning entirely like any other, Charlie Fish got up and did the things he needed to do, in the order he needed to do them.

Except it wasn't a Thursday morning like any other any more.

He hid for a while in the playlist. He was coming to the end of the sixties and he put King Curtis in there, Aretha Franklin and Arthur Conley, Canned Heat and The Band, Jimmy Cliff and Archie Bell. Marvin Gaye heard it on the grapevine, Bowie sang Space Oddity, and the Stones sang Gimme Shelter. There never was, thought Charlie, any shelter then, and there was surely none now.

He walked down the road to Sadiq's store. The shopfront windows had all been put in. Sadiq had got the frames boarded up and then opened for business as usual, early in the morning for the papers. He hadn't had much sleep. He said to Charlie, "I want to thank you, you and the others who came out last night. I'd have been up to your house but I'm sorry, I've not had time."

"No problem," said Charlie, "you've had it all to do. Are your wife and kids OK?"

"They're alright, yes. My wife's shaken up, you can imagine, and really angry too. Fucking yobs. Can you believe those people?"

"I'm afraid I can. It's getting worse, isn't it?"

"It's not the country I grew up in, that's for sure."

"Me neither."

"Charlie - I do really mean it, I thank you. You nearly got your head kicked in there."

Charlie said it was nothing, any neighbour would do it, he wasn't the only one that came out. He was doing calm and polite on the outside, and inside he was working overtime, trying to piece together what had happened. It was, he thought, an irony that he'd spent thirty years in and out of alcoholic blackout, and yet now he was sober he struggled to remember anything from one day to the next. He wondered, if he could just see the present without the future getting in the way all the time, would that make it easier? Then Sadiq said, "That Molly though, she's really something. It was touch and go before she showed up."

"She took me home, one of them must have clocked me, I wasn't seeing straight. What did she do?"

"They were after the booze, obviously. They were pissed up already but people came out when they heard the glass go in, so then it was all push and shove in the street. Handbags really, but threatening to get worse. They lamped a couple of people, you got some, I saw that - then I was in the doorway and they were coming back at me when she got here. She came and stood next to me and she just told them, they better leave it and they better go home now. She's just one girl, there was four or five of them - and it was amazing. Her voice, it was like super-clear. She just stood there and everything shut up. You heard her and you thought, yeah, that's it now. They'll be going. And they did. Like they'd all been told off by their Mums. I almost laughed. Mind you, Mums or no Mums, I know a couple of those toe-rags. They'll not be coming back. They're fucking toast."

Charlie's head swam to and fro listening to him. Urban living in the times of austerity - a thing of such charm and style and grace, absolutely not. And now Molly was The Thief Whisperer … well, that part didn't surprise him. Far as he knew, she had infinite capability. If he'd looked up and seen her flying past with a blue cape flapping on her back, he'd have shrugged and thought, well guess what now.

He shook hands with Sadiq and told him to take care, and Sadiq told Charlie to do the same. Then Charlie set off walking to the hospital. It seemed to him by now entirely reasonable that, on top of violent burglary, the breakdown of civil society, the disintegration of the food chain, the daily presence in his life of the devil, and the end of the world on Sunday, he should also be getting the results of a prostate biopsy. Who wants a quiet life, after all?

* * *

All Charlie's life he had been trying to make sense of it - a doomed project, it now seemed, along the lines of trying to wrestle with a jellyfish. In his early years he had made no headway at all, but then alcohol stepped in and suddenly, as soon as he had a drink inside him, everything made perfect sense. This proved to be an illusion, but by then it was too late. Since by then it had become impossible to stop drinking, it had also become necessary to continue living in the illusion. So he did.

For a while, he had some success with another device - he tried making sense of life by writing about it. He'd started doing this when he was seven, beginning with the nightmare he'd had about the rising of the sea and the devil's appearance in his garden, bearing promises and threats. He would do great things, he'd been told. What did that mean? Would it seem more clear if he wrote it down?

Soon he was writing everything down. Dreams, thoughts, images, whatever bubbled up from the morass between his ears, he wrote it all down. It seemed to him a natural thing to do - words flowed onto paper for him with the same ready ease as water from a tap - and for a long while, he thought he was doing nothing unusual or exceptional. He assumed that everybody could write, and he couldn't at all understand it when he found that they could not.

Writing was, like alcohol, a release and a relief. The orchestra forever tuning up in his head, that scratching, perma-scraping racket of discordant nerve-ends - writing hushed it, it made him the conductor, it ordered and arranged it. People began to read what he wrote, and to say kind things about it. He began to say that it was fiction, and they bought that idea. He began to buy the idea himself, and to believe that he would be a Great Novelist. Had he not been promised great things?

He wrote his first novel when he was nineteen. It was rubbish from start to finish. If Samuel Beckett had been illiterate, talentless, and completely stoned day and night, his output might have read something like Charlie's first attempt, albeit not nearly so bad.

He wrote his second novel when he was twenty-two. It was better, but still not good enough. Then, when he twenty-five, something happened. He had spent three years working as a copywriter for an advertising agency, which may on the one hand have meant that he was telling fibs to flog tat for a living, but on the other hand it meant that he had to learn discipline. Clients didn't pay to have words in their ads that didn't work for them, and Charlie realised that words in his Great Novels had to start working rather harder as well. So, when he could bear the rising din between his ears no longer and he had to have another mental clear-out, he left his job and flew to Morocco. This time, he thought, I'll get it right.

He sat at the bar in Heathrow, drinking margaritas because he was a sophisticated young man. You could still get on a plane drunk in those days, and indeed Charlie for many years would never get on one sober. There was a tall, strikingly handsome man on the barstool next to him, and they struck up airport conversation as you do. Destinations, reasons for travel, preferred airlines, worst airline food ever, best beaches, best nightclubs, so forth - casual topics from a lost world, when Charlie looks back on it now.

He said he was heading for Morocco to write a novel, and the other man got a glint in his eye. "I believe," he said, "that's going to go well for you. Remember I said so, won't you?" He patted Charlie on the arm and the touch of his palm was hot, with a light charge like static electricity.

Then he got up to go, saying his flight was being called. Later Charlie realised, the man had told him nothing of who he was, where he was going or what he did. Then the meeting dropped away into the mist of the margaritas, just as so many other things for thirty years fell away into fog.

He flew to Casablanca, took a train to Rabat, and wrote a novel in bright sunshine on the pale blue roof of a cheap hotel. He wrote it in two weeks flat, and he knew it would be published. He had found his voice - and his voice was vicious. The novel was violent, venomous, vitriolic. It was a satirical assault on Thatcher and all her works, on the world we had already become and the world we were yet going to be. Then, as now, Charlie believed he saw two truths. There was what was in front of you, which was bad enough - and then there was what was beneath and behind it, waiting to crawl out. That was worse by far, and it was coming soon.

Back in London he was given a contract and an advance, and - his reaction to this news being as in all matters wildly disproportionate - he immediately fancied himself a cross between George Orwell, Charles Dickens, and Joe Strummer. He also believed that as soon as the novel came out, no one would ever vote Conservative again.

Well, that didn't happen. The novel was what the trade likes to term 'critically acclaimed' - a necessary phrase to be deployed when virtually no one's actually bought a book, but it's had a few half-decent reviews.

Charlie spent a fair period of time boiling internally with agony and resentment. How was he not being showered with love and banknotes? The failure of the universe to recognise his almighty talent was a rejection almost too bitter to be borne. Of course he showed this inner writhing to no one, and instead played the part around town of The New Young Novelist. This involved getting commissions from magazines to fly around the world writing travel stories, and going to parties in clubs and offices where you proved with effortless nonchalance your ability to take your drink and your drugs better than that other New Young Novelist over there who'd fallen over in the corner, and who would therefore not be getting the ticket to Miami that you coveted yourself. Because, actually, you'd spiked his drink, the uppity talentless little shit.

Charlie made money for a while - glossy, vacuous money for writing air-headed puff, but money all the same. As time passed, however, a significant issue crept over the horizon, drawing steadily nearer, looming ever larger and more ominous: The Second Novel.

He absolutely could not write it. He tried drinking and writing it, and he tried not drinking and writing it. He tried smoking dope and writing it. He tried snorting coke and writing it. He tried writing it in Wisconsin, and he tried writing it in Nicaragua. He tried writing it on a Greek island, and he tried writing it in a Welsh cottage - and wherever and however he tried to write it, it always turned out that he had nothing to write, and he had nothing to say.

The horror. He was going to be a Great Novelist … and now he was a journalist.

Then the magazines grew less interested in giving him commissions. After all, who was he any more? Who had he ever been? And Charlie became less interested in staying upright at parties. After all, who the fuck were these people anyway?

These people grew up and got married and had children and mortgages. Charlie didn't. Charlie went to the pub. Men used to say, that Charlie Fish, he was a proper success with the women. Now they looked at him and thought, how was it successful with women, that no relationship you were in ever lasted for longer than a fortnight?

He left London. He couldn't afford to live there, and he couldn't handle people seeing him there. He knew everyone knew he was a failure. He said he was going away to write the next novel, but in his heart he knew there wasn't one. There wasn't even a next paragraph.

He was someone who might have been someone, and now he wasn't anyone at all, and he was doing his first geographical. Over time, he did a string of them. He went to this town and then to that one, and he went to this woman and then to that one, and then he always moved on again because wherever he went, his head kept coming too. He wrote less and less for the papers and the magazines until he wrote nothing at all, and he got a job in a supermarket, and if he wasn't in the supermarket he was in The Laughing Dog.

Looking back now as he walked to the hospital, the whole business brought to mind what he reckoned to be the greatest joke in the history of mankind. It came from - where else? - an episode of The Simpsons, in which Marge becomes a best-selling novelist. Then she catches Homer out in a lie, and confronts him on it. Poor Homer cries out - with that perfectly realised, childlike combination of guilt, bafflement, and affronted inspiration - "I wasn't lying! I was writing fiction with my mouth!"

On another level though, Charlie wondered if he'd ever written fiction at all. The way he saw things, behind the addled vanity of his brief and tawdry career, he'd been telling the truth all along. He'd been saying What Was Really Going On. He'd wanted to be a writer because he'd wanted to go up to the world and shake it by the shoulders and yell in its face, "Look around you! Look what's happening! We're all going to die and we're all going to hell!"

So, he realised, he hadn't just been thinking that this week. He'd been thinking it all along - and he accepted, of course, that it was unsurprising therefore that his writing career had been brief. From the publishing industry's point of view, he really wasn't delivering what you'd deem a commercially viable storyline:

You're All Going To Die!!!!!

But hey, it was true. Indeed, it was going to happen on Sunday. On Sunday we were all going to die, and we were all going to hell. Unless, of course, we were there already.

Charlie walked on. The heat and humidity were borderline unbearable, like wading through damp, boiled cotton wool. He shook his head. It made no sense. It was February. He felt the shimmy happening, the air becoming mirage, the roiling upset behind his eyes like an earthquake in a ploughed field, his brain like mud turning fluid, finding a new wavelength. He looked about him in the burning street, hardly anyone about, no traffic, what few souls there were all scurrying, head down, not looking. Don't look, don't look - he knew how they felt. They wanted everything to be alright, that was all - who wouldn't? He didn't want anything different. He was one of us, whether he felt like it or he didn't, and what did we want?

We wanted light and warmth and safe food and good health. We wanted clean water, and we wanted weather that didn't kill us. We wanted to be secure, and we didn't want to hear that we weren't. We didn't want to know that the climate was changing, or that the economy was tanking, or that we lived in a society that didn't know what to do about it. If we weren't safe that meant we would die, and then we were scared and we needed someone to blame. Then we looked at the refugees, and we didn't want to know that they were refugees because they could no longer live where they'd been born, because the places they'd been born had become scorched, war-torn, uninhabitable deserts. We looked at them clamouring at the gates, pressed against the fencing with their fingers knotted through the wire, scuttling through tunnels and clinging to lorries and tramping through fields and down train tracks and frightening us with their desperation. We saw them dying in airless containers, we saw them drowning by the thousand, and instead of calling them refugees we called them migrants. We felt them pressing on our space, leaning on our dwindling resources, and we hated them because they shamed us because we didn't help them, because we wanted them to die instead of us. We hated them because we didn't want to know that what was happening there might all too soon be happening here. We hated them because we knew things really weren't alright, they weren't alright at all, and we were scared at the way things were falling apart, and we knew we were going to die.

Mind you, Charlie thought it oddly misplaced to be scared of dying. The way he saw it, dying wasn't the problem. It was living was the hard part.

He wondered what a psychiatrist would make of it. He'd gone a few rounds with a couple of them in the past, but neither side had ever gotten very far. A psychiatrist might well, he knew, have suggested that Charlie and reality weren't the most close-knit of partners - and being an alky, Charlie might well have suggested that the psychiatrist go fuck himself.

* * *

The notion that as you grew older you grew wiser was, he felt, plainly nonsense. It was of course possible that the rest of the species were all ahead of him on that, and were all turning steadily into saints and sages, though on the evidence he couldn't see it. As far as his own carcass and character went, however, it seemed the only thing about him showing any sign of growth was his prostate.

Charlie tried hard to see the funny side. For a start, the male reproductive and urinary system was clear proof not only that God existed, but also that he had a sense of humour. The whole construction was so absurdly complex that neither evolution nor intelligent design seemed remotely adequate as explanations. Only Design By Practical Joker fit the bill, and Charlie had become - literally - the butt of the joke.

He had spent a fair proportion of the last few months on the brink of incontinence. It was often inconvenient, occasionally painful, and meant that he only rarely slept for more than a few hours at a time. On the plus side, it did at least make sense of the adverts in the gents at motorway service stations.

It was a long time since Charlie had driven anywhere much, whether on a motorway or otherwise, but those ads had haunted him for years, filling him with pity for the poor souls who had to write them. Nowhere else in the public domain did the hype industry feel free to shout at you about Urine Leakage. Not on bus shelters or billboards, not on the radio or in the cinema - nowhere. Urine Leakage was the Male Dark Secret, a subject only to be spoken of in the gents on the motorway. Along with van hire, obviously. Indeed, if motorway service stations were to be believed, the principal purpose of the modern male was to drive a rented van, and to wet his pants in it.

The only other place you talked about Urine Leakage was at the doctor's surgery. That, however, presupposed that you could get into such a place, and that you could find a doctor to talk to once you had. Now that we lived in North Korea, Charlie had found, these were not such easy things to achieve. In what little remained of the National Health Service, steadily gutted of its staff in the wake of England's glorious isolation, treatment now largely consisted of hanging on a telephone or sitting in a waiting room until you had either cured yourself or died.

In short, Charlie reckoned that going to the NHS these days required an anaesthetic before you'd even got through the door. The service was collapsing because we gave it no money, and because we had vigorously made unwelcome all the Asians, Africans, and Europeans who had kept it going. And yet, still the idiot management felt it necessary to plaster the place with posters telling us that they cared, and asking for our feedback. Charlie's feedback would have been simple - stop telling me you care, and just do it. And stop wasting money on stupid posters when you could spend it on staff who, you never know, might actually help me not to die.

Charlie's views on death - whether it should be coming this Sunday, or at some later date if the devil decided to reschedule - were, like his views on pretty much everything, contradictory, eccentric, and polemical. In a nutshell, however, he actually wasn't bothered about dying.

He had faith. True, in the past week his line to God seemed to have broken up, leaving him when he dialled in with nothing but silence and static. True, this was frustrating and alarming, and he would have appreciated it if God had installed an answering service. "Hi, this is heaven. We're sorry but all our operators are busy, as we are experiencing a heavy volume of calls at the moment. Your call is important to us, and we apologise for the wait. Please hold the line and an advisor will be with you as soon as possible. You are currently number 4,758,922 in the queue. For customers concerned about recent rumours regarding the end of the world, our press statement can be found online at …"

Actually it can't, Charlie remembered, now the devil had broken the internet - but he still had faith. He believed that he would not die, but merely move to a better place where cars never had flat tyres, where DVD players never broke, where the devil did not bring you outrageous fake tax demands, where thugs and bigots did not attack your neighbours, where your prostate caused you no grief, and where a superbly comfortable viewing gallery with a truly excellent coffee bar would have a coin-operated hyper-version of the Hubble telescope mounted at exactly your personal eye-level so you could look out and gaze upon infinity while snacking on an almond croissant.

And that was just purgatory! That was just the reception centre while you filled in the paperwork to get to the real thing!

So, death - his own death - didn't worry Charlie. It was going to be alright. He would prefer it not to involve pain, but if it did, then so it goes. He would just have to tell himself that pain was the touchstone of spiritual progress, and grit his teeth.

The death of everything and everybody on the planet, however, was a different matter. True, it was hard not to think that there were a few who had it coming to them. True, when it came to the debriefing, we'd have to confess that we hadn't exactly distinguished ourselves in the Good Behaviour column. True, Charlie wasn't a great fan of being around people in general - but it wasn't their fault he didn't fit in. He didn't want them all to die.

In sum, it was a bit harsh - and that devil, really, what was his problem? Couldn't he just don a nice velvet smoking jacket and put his feet up and torture the souls he had already? Had he not collected enough of them by now? That guy - he was just more more more, me me me, all that resentment and dissatisfaction and blame - it was so familiar, Charlie wearily realised. The devil's problem was, he was all too human.

He was nearing the hospital. He squared his shoulders and made ready to push through the throngs of the sick, the lost, the untreated. One thing was for sure, if the end of the world came, the NHS definitely wouldn't cope with it. The NHS was over already.

* * *

The consultant told him the biopsy was negative.

Excellent, thought Charlie, the world's going to end but never mind, I don't have cancer.

"However," the consultant said, "just because the biopsy's negative doesn't mean you don't have cancer."

Charlie thought about the last few months. He'd sat in waiting rooms for so long that the devil could have ended the world ten times over while he was in there, plus started it up all over again, plus started a new spare world on the side for fun. He'd pissed in buckets. He'd had blood tests. He'd lain on his side while doctors shoved their fingers up his arse, along with blunt instruments and hey, for all he knew a plumber's toolkit, a wardrobe, a watermelon and a willow tree. Then they'd splayed him out like a crab and fired needles up inside him. This hurt so much, it made the Spanish Inquisition look like Morecambe &

Wise. On balance, Charlie felt by now that it would be nice to have learnt something.

So," he said, "after all that, you still don't know if I have cancer or not."

"I don't. The biopsy says you don't, but the symptoms and the blood tests and the examinations say you do."

Ten needles, thought Charlie. I could barely walk when you were done. Ten fucking needles. Did you miss?

He asked, "So what do we do now?"

"I'm going to put you on medication for four months to shrink the gland. Then we'll look again. If you find in the pharmacy that they've run out of the drugs I'm prescribing, I'm sorry but that's the way it is. You'll just have to hunt around. There'll be a chemist somewhere in town who has them.   And in case you weren't aware, the system of prescription charges has been abolished. The prices are market rate now, for everyone. Good luck, come back in four months, and don't trip over any dead people on your way out."

"Did you really just say that?"

"I did. I work for the NHS. It's a joke. The NHS is a joke, I mean. What I said, that part was serious."

"Oh well," said Charlie, "the world ends on Sunday, so it doesn't really matter anyway."

"Excellent," said the consultant, "that'll be a weight off all our minds. Would you like to see a psychiatrist while you're here?"

"Would I get to see one before Sunday?"

"You'll be lucky if you get to see one this year."

"I won't bother, thanks. Last time I saw someone about my mental health, they asked me if I ever thought about harming myself. I laughed. I said I wasn't suicidal, it was much worse than that. They looked nervous and said they wanted to increase the dose on my anti-depressants. I said if I thought drugs would solve the problem, I'd go see a proper dealer. I said it was a spiritual problem. They looked at me like I was mad. I thought that was pretty stupid. How else would you look at me?"

"Alright," said the consultant, "enough. There's thousands of people out there. Most of them are just English, but some of them may even be sick. So get out."

I don't like your bedside manner."

"You're not in bed. So clear off. Oh, and this end of the world business. Can a person make an advance booking?"

* * *

Charlie went to the psychiatric unit. He wasn't going there for himself, but to find out about his friend from The Sanity Club who'd started drinking again. The unit was supposed to be secure, but it wasn't. Someone had smashed in the keypad for the electronic lock, and the door stood ajar. Charlie wandered in, the doorway a ruined portal into worlds that had travelled far, far away from any he'd ever inhabited himself. Patients lay motionless in their beds, some twisted into unlikely, angular shapes. Others walked about, conducting unintelligible conversations with themselves. Some sat in chairs or on their beds, fiddling aimlessly with random possessions. The place was filthy. Uneaten food lay about on trays, and the floor was dotted with random litter and paperwork.

Charlie looked for someone who might be caring for these people, but he couldn't find anyone. He checked every bed, every curtained-off space, but his friend didn't seem to be there. Finally in the corridor outside he found a junior doctor, who would have hurtled straight past him had Charlie not just stood in his way. He agreed reluctantly to go with Charlie to the abandoned nurses' station by the entrance to the ward, and rummaged through files and folders and clipboards looking for the name Charlie gave him.

It seemed Charlie's mate had come in, raved for forty-eight hours, and then discharged himself. The doctor flipped through the notes and said, "Looks like he wasn't safe to go, but they didn't stop him because he wasn't safe to stay either. Looks like he was seriously insane."

"What, and everybody else here is seriously sane?"

"No, everybody else here is seriously sedated. God help us when we run out of drugs for this lot. But your mate, he refused all medication. He said the devil was after him and he needed to stay alert."

"Well, you would need to stay alert, wouldn't you?"

I'm not kidding, he was barking."

"He's an alky with a drink in him, of course he's barking. But hey, don't worry about it. The world ends on Sunday, so he can go to heaven and it'll all be cool."

The world ends on Sunday? Superb. I work for the NHS, I've been sleeping in my car, and I haven't been paid for three months. So even if they send me to hell, it has to be better than this."

* * *

Charlie walked home and got his bike out. His friend on the relapse was called Jim, and he was known at The Sanity Club as Jimmy Why Me, because he never understood why not. He lived fifteen minutes' ride away in a two-up two-down like Charlie's, and Charlie rode there now to see if he was there, and if there was anything he could do for him if he was.

He found the front door open. He knocked and got no answer, so he went on in. The living room looked like Godzilla had spent the night there with his mates, eating takeout pizza and drinking the local store dry. The place was littered with super-strength lager cans, overflowing ashtrays, and uneaten cheese feast stuffed crust in scattered boxes. The TV had been left on, and a frozen image of a jabbering moron in a reality show gurned at the empty, half-dark room. Charlie was surprised not to find Jim on the sofa amid the debris, either unconscious or close to it - for an alky on the binge actually to make it upstairs to bed suggested an unusual degree of planning and effort. So he went upstairs, but Jim wasn't there either.

The mess didn't faze him. Over the past ten years, Charlie had learnt that alkies on a relapse plunge back to the worst of their drinking with dizzying rapidity. You could be sober ten, fifteen, twenty-five years, it didn't matter - you picked up the first drink, and then you hurtled downhill like you'd never been away. The illness welcomed you back with open arms. Oh yes, it crooned, come here my baby … so you didn't start over from scratch. You started where you'd left off, and you raced in a tearing hurry from there to discover new lows. Alkies, Charlie thought, were explorers. As resolute adventurers had opened up paths into Africa and the Amazon, so alkies with grim determination charted new regions of squalor and degradation.

And it could be me, thought Charlie. On any day, it could be me.

A friend told him once of an alky who drank again after two decades sober. In a fortnight from the first drink, they dismantled their entire life - job gone, marriage gone, the lot. And while Charlie was dismayed at the news, inside there was the knowing voice that asked, A fortnight? What took you so long?

Neither of the bedrooms had been slept in. Finding no sign of life, Charlie came back downstairs and went to look in the kitchen. It was strewn with cans and bottles and detritus like the living room. The door to the basement was open, so Charlie went to have a look down there.

Jim was hanging from the exposed beam across the centre of the cellar. He'd got a length of rope, tied it firm around his neck and the beam, then kicked away the chair he'd been standing on. A near-empty vodka bottle lay sideways on the floor by the chair. Jim's tongue stuck thick and purple from his mouth, and dried foam ran down his chin. The room smelt of shit and piss.

Charlie turned to go back upstairs, to get away from the body, and found Luke barring his way. Luke told him, "That one's mine now. Don't you think it's about time you joined him? My house has many chambers, and I've a room just for you. Well-stocked drinks cabinet, plush soft furnishings, adult channels on the telly, everything a boy needs for an agreeable eternity."

Charlie pushed past him to get out of the basement. He was too sick and angry to speak, until Luke followed him up to the kitchen, put a hand on his shoulder and turned him round, forcing him to face him.

So Charlie told him, "You know what? I went to hospital today. It's falling apart, obviously, what with it being the end of the world and all, but never mind that. I saw a doctor and he told me I might have cancer. So here's the thing. You're stood there now, you jumped-up little misery merchant - well, you offer me a choice between cancer and a drink, you go on. You offer me that, and what d'you think I'll take? I'll tell you now. I'll take cancer. I'll take cancer because maybe they can fix it and maybe they can't, but either way it is what it is. Whereas a drink - that's cancer of the soul, and that's what you've got. You're Soul Cancer Mary, you are, and I'm not having it. So I've told you before and I'll tell you again, you can fuck off. Fuck off out of my face, fuck off out of my life. I don't care how many or how few days of it there are left, every time you come after me I'll tell you the same. Because you just don't get it. You think I go to The

Sanity Club and I don't know about funerals? You think another funeral's going to make me drink? I hate to disappoint you. We can do the big things, us alkies. Death, bereavement, divorce, cancer, we can do all that stuff. We like the drama and we like straightening our shoulders and we like taking it on the chin and we like digging deep and getting through. And I'm getting through. So do what you want, pal. I'm not yours, clear? Not now, not ever. End of message. And excuse me, but I have to make a phone call now. I believe we still have emergency services in this country, and while we do I'd like to use them."

Charlie got out his mobile and rang 999. Luke watched him, looking thoughtful and amused. When Charlie was done on the phone Luke said to him, "You have to forgive me. I'm on a learning curve here. So let me get this right. You can take a dead body, you can take cancer, you can take violence in the street, you can take the society you live in going to the dogs. OK, I get this. Tell me though, what happens if your coffee pot explodes? What happens if your toothbrush snaps, or you break a shoelace? I'm just thinking aloud here."

He sauntered out of the house as if he'd done no more than drop by for a cup of tea.

The nonchalance was an act, though. This wretched planet - if something didn't change in a hurry, it was really going to ruin his career.

＊ ＊ ＊

Middle management was hell.

Luke sat at the bar in The Laughing Dog and considered his situation. It had been getting worse all week, and the prospects for improvement any time soon seemed dim indeed. On a scale of one to ten, he was going to miss his targets by billions.

He was the Regional Operations Manager for Hades Inc, and he ought to have been seriously pleased about it. He had multiple galaxies answering to him, with main branches and local convenience outlets established in all the major systems, selling happiness and reaping souls wherever the trade was there to be done. In theory, if he made it work and he hit the numbers, he was just a couple of steps away from a directorship. There were eager junior managers all over the cosmos who'd have sold their own motherboards to be in the spot he had - and yet he cursed the day they'd offered it to him.

Of all the planets in all the solar systems in all the galaxies in all the universe, his region had to include this one - this Earth, this prostate gland of a planet, this lunatic asylum. In all his long and varied career, through millions upon millions of years, nowhere ever had he come across a species so absolutely unwilling to get with the programme. Or worse - some of them didn't even resist it, they just up and plain ignored it. They said they were too busy doing something else. They said they were Quakers, or surfers, or birdwatchers. He'd stand there telling them he was the devil and they were all like, yeah, whatever.

Of course he told them he was the devil. There was a frisson in playing the part, obviously, but the idea was to scare them. "I represent the devil, let me give you my card" - somehow that didn't have the same ring. Middle management all over the universe played the same game, they said they were the main man, they bigged themselves up that way. It was time-honoured practice. It made you feel good, it made The Boss look omnipresent, and it made the customers happy because they thought they were getting top-level personal attention - so everyone was a winner.

Besides, they didn't actually want to meet The Boss, not the real boss, not really. The Boss might put them off a tad, what with being huge and made of lava and covered in flames. He gets out a tissue to blow his nose, your whole solar system's ash before the deal's even done. That might be a tad brand-damaging. So for safety's sake, The Boss was what you might call hands-off - and, naturally, he made a positive out of it. He encouraged his people to go out and develop themselves, he was a big investor in Demon Resources, he drove everyone hard to stay upbeat and on-message.

Happiness - that was the point, right? What was Hades Inc for, if not to peddle happiness? Obviously you had to mine the stuff from somewhere - no one gets energy for free, do they? - so you cooked, flayed, froze, sandblasted and otherwise reduced many souls to a rich bloody jus in the power plants of hell to generate the end product - but the deal was a fair one. Everyone bought it - except for this one fucking stupid unfathomable rock here, where there were actually people who told him to his face that happiness wasn't the point. Damn, he could scream, he could puke, he could tear his liver out and eat it in public, it was just so indescribably ridiculous.

That Charlie Fish, for one. Fish had actually told him, to his face, that a person couldn't be happy all the time - that life didn't work that way. He said you didn't pray for outcomes, you prayed for the strength to deal with whatever the outcome might be. And what sort of bunny-hugging horseshit was that? What sort of lettuce-munching invertebrate spouted tosh like that?

The alkies were bad, but they were far from the only ones. There were the schizophrenics and the depressives and the bipolar bunch - they were all hard to reach. And then, there was just the obscenely prolific variety of the place. Even if people purported to be sane (which very often they really weren't) they were always up to something. They were gardening or baking or jogging or collecting Doctor Who memorabilia. They were yachting or playing darts or doing yoga. They were tweeting or being famous or sitting in their bedroom hacking into the Pentagon. They were making playlists. Whatever they were doing, they weren't selling him their souls. Why couldn't they just lie about and eat and sleep and fuck like everybody else? Everybody else just waved from their divans and their mud baths, yeah, sure, soul, have that, I got no use for it, no problem. But this lot - hoarders, doubters, nitpickers, hair-splitters - they weren't trading.

So what was he supposed to do? Go around eight billion of them personally, with the paperwork for each one, give them incentives and inducements and get down on his knees and plead? What was he, Santa Claus? Did they not realise he was in a volume business here? Did they not realise, if this planet didn't yield like the budget said it should, his numbers would have a hole in them bigger than the Horsehead Nebula?

He stared glumly at his beer on the bar top. He told himself, The bottom line, Lukey boy, is you are so screwed. He would go back to head office after this, his Performance Development Review would be an epic fail that'd go down as legendary in the annals of the corporation - he blew a whole planet! - and he'd spend the rest of eternity grilling slowly on a skewer.

Well, he thought, looking at his hands, at least I won't have to wear this horrible flesh kit much longer. Man, it itches. Mind you, the beer did help, he had to admit. Get some of that inside you, it was almost tolerable pretending to be human. He held his pint glass up, and studied it in the murky light of the Dog. On his return, he thought, he could at least report back that alcohol was one of the corporation's more effective products. Booze, he thought, was a project they should really get behind cosmos-wide.

The landlord watched Luke admiring his pint. There were, as ever, only a few customers, regulars whose need for social interaction was minimal. The Dog was ordinarily a place for steady, determined drinking in an unbroken, dismal silence - but, since Luke was a new customer, something not seen hereabouts in years or quite possibly centuries, and dimly remembering that business required him to be host-like, the landlord told Luke that the beer was a guest ale. He explained that he got three such ales in every other Thursday. The idea, he continued, was you looked at the alcohol-by-volume percentage on the labels on the hand pumps, and whichever of the three had the most alcohol in it, if you were a regular of the Dog, then that was the one you drank. It didn't matter if it tasted like engine oil. The idea was to get sodden as quickly as possible. Why else would you drink in the Dog?

"Right," muttered a motionless figure a couple of yards along the bar, "who the fuck would want to be in here sober?"

"Would it interest you to know," said Luke, "that the world ends on Sunday?"

The bloke along the bar asked, "What time?"

"What do you mean, what time?"

"I mean will I have to start drinking early, fuckwit. What d'you think I mean?"

"Yeah," said the landlord. "That'd be shit, having to open early on a Sunday."

Luke despaired. He said, just for form's sake, "I don't suppose either of you would be interested in selling me your soul?"

"Nah mate, sorry. My ex-wife's got it."

"Really? What does she do with it?"

"Sticks pins in it, I should imagine. What would you want with it anyway? It's not in very good condition."

"Well, I'm the devil. So I'd torment it for all eternity."

"Fair enough. Be like drinking in here then." At which point, the customer and the landlord had the best laugh they'd had since about 1973.

"Actually," said Luke, "I'm going to be honest here. Can I speak in confidence?"

"Say what you like, mate," the landlord told him. "We won't remember a word."

Luke took a deep breath and confessed. He said, "I'm not really the devil. I'm just his henchman. I'm the hired help. I just manage the local area."

To his surprise, and his considerable interest, he felt a great relief, as if he'd lifted the weight of millennia off his shoulders. He took a long swig of beer, and wondered what that was all about.

The landlord asked him, "Been doing that job long then?"

"Too long," said Luke, "you have no idea. And looking back, I was an absolute fool. I was just a young string of code, really green. I did a good job for them on the community programme, going round signing up backward civilisations. You'd have to stand there being all nice while some pack of imbecile lungfish slathered and drooled around your feet. You'd string 'em a line about the Hades Inc commitment to developing new worlds, all that. Then you'd sign 'em up and bingo, more soul food. We're like FIFA, only in space. So then management came and told me all about my potential, said I should be a team leader. Only bought it, didn't I? And I've been eating, sleeping, dreaming the damn company ever since. Cut me, I bleed hellfire. Makes you wonder who's sold whose soul to whom, if you get me. And it's hard to say that with some beer inside you, eh?"

"Sounds like you could use a break."

"I should never have stepped up. I should have stayed on the shop floor. I could be clocking in, doing my shift, working that pitchfork, clocking out. No pressure. Put in an honest day's torment, go home, watch I'm A Demon Get Me Out Of Here. Instead of which I'm in The Laughing Dog, a billion light years from anywhere, staying in a Travelodge and wondering what the hell happened. You turn around one day and where's your life gone, eh?"

"Know the feeling mate. Still, won't matter after Sunday, will it?"

"It won't matter for you. I'll still be here, won't I? Running the numbers, writing the reports. Oh well, best be off." He sighed deeply. "A bloke needs to sleep properly when he's preparing an apocalypse."

Luke said goodnight, and left the landlord and his customer supping their engine oil. After he was out the door the landlord said, "Well, he's not from round here, is he?"

"End of the world my arse," said the customer. "He's from fucking outer space, that one."

Luke - having the exceptionally sharp ears that come with being an emissary of the devil - heard every word crystal clear, though he was already halfway down the street. To be who he was, the Big I Am, and yet to be on a planet that so consistently failed to take him seriously - it was baffling, galling, and enraging in equal measure. Right, he thought. The first place that fries is The Laughing Dog.

* * *

"Tough day," said Molly. "How are you bearing up, old geezer?"

She'd come round after her shift and found him buried in the playlist. She wasn't sure that Iggy Pop and The Stooges were a shining example of the peaks of human cultural achievement, but a little ranting shouty darkness on the soundtrack seemed excusable in the circumstances.

"I'm not doing so bad," said Charlie. "Yelling at the devil made me feel a bit better."

"How did he take it?"

"Hard to say, I wasn't paying attention, I was ringing an ambulance. It's amazing, we actually still have some. Anyway, I think he might be sulking. It seems I'm not doing what he wants."

"Good for you. Do you really believe he's the devil?"

"You tell me. You're smarter than I am."

"Well," said Molly, "there's several ways of looking at it. You could be mentally ill, which would be a surprise to no one who knows you and cares for you. You could be the canary in the coal mine, the scout that goes ahead, the man cursed with the gift of prophecy. You could simply be right in every detail. Or it could be all of the above. Shouldn't you ask your sponsor?"

"I'm going to look a bit of a berk when we all wake up and go to work on Monday, aren't I?"

"Well, it'll be better looking a berk than being dead. But whatever happens, I'd like you to know something. When my Dad was dying, you looked after me. You taught me to cook. You bought me school uniform, which occasionally was even the right size. You came along when I got my exam results. You gave me your spare bedroom, you did all that. So you need to know I'll always remember it, and you need to know I love you."

Charlie looked at her smiling at him, trying to hold back the tears in his eyes. He thought, there's a power greater than me, and it's in this room right now.

* * *

He burnt a couple more CD's, and handed her the latest instalments of the playlist. He told her he'd made it into the seventies. Molly said she loved what he was doing and The Staple Singers, Bill Withers, Isaac Hayes, she was absolutely in favour. On the other hand, she told him, great as they are, he had way too many Rolling Stones songs. Charlie said there was no such thing as too many Rolling Stones songs, not from that time.

He said if he got as far as Ziggy Stardust and the first Roxy Music album before the devil did his thing and they all went up in flames, then at least the playlist would have entered the modern age.

He defined the beginning of the modern age as the moment when he, Charlie Fish, had bought his first albums - on the grounds, obviously, that the modern age couldn't possibly have got under way without him. He'd had a summer job on the forecourt of a garage, and he'd spent his first wages on music. He'd bought five albums mail order from an ad in the back of New Musical Express, and two of them were by David Bowie - Ziggy Stardust and Aladdin Sane.

He readily admitted that he'd prefer to draw a veil over the other three. Two of them were by preposterous prog rock titans Yes. The third was by a long-forgotten Welsh band called Man. He could remember nothing about it whatsoever, except obviously that the lyrics were Shakespearean in their profundity.

He told her that with the wages from the garage, he'd also bought his first personally selected, fashion-statement clothes. He'd bought a cheesecloth shirt, and a pair of mustard yellow loon pants. They were made of some kind of velveteen. They were chemically-enhanced post-hippy trousers.

"Oh," she swooned, "you must have been such a dashing boy."

"I was outrageous. My hair actually went over my collar."

"I'm surprised you made it out of Hampshire alive, being so far ahead of the game there."

"Oh I've always been cutting edge, me. I don't just see the future, I live in it."

"You want to give me the forecast then?"

"The devil ends the world. We go out into the street and there's no one left. There's just you, me, and a very good soundtrack."

Molly told him, "You want to be careful what you wish for."

- Boing!

- And a good morning to you too, B. The sun rises for us around the rim of this paste diamond of a world, with its belching power plants and its scenic burning forests, its once wondrous bleached corals and its fan-assisted oven of an atmosphere, and it heralds the moment when we are but forty-eight hours from rendering the place lifeless. So what is boing? Are you Zebedee now?

- Am I who?

- I've been compiling the cultural archive for Demon U before we wipe. The playlist's in there, obviously, but you should see some of the other stuff these people have come up with. Zebedee's a tiny bad guy on a coiled spring in The Magic Roundabout, I most earnestly recommend it. You may identify with him. Then there's Roobarb And Custard, The Clangers, and Noggin The Nog. Genius all of it. But tell me, what is boing?

- Boing is the proof that I too am a genius. I've outpaced all your cosmologists, all your astrophysicists, all your churning mainframes, and I've come up with a Unified Theory Of Everything. Not only that, but it's a unified theory that can be expressed in one word: Boing.

- Pray expand, my ancient binary co-worker. Enlarge for me, dilate and expound.

- Big Bang. Pop fizz hot hot hot whoosh. Everything flies outwards. Then eventually, at first slowly, as matter reaches its braking distance, cosmos-wide gravity starts exerting a reverse attraction. Everything starts falling back towards where it came from. Faster and faster it falls, get your hard hat on, Big Crunch. We're all violently condensed back into the dot we first sprang from. Rest a while, repeat. Hence, the universe is elastic. It's an extremely big rubber band. Hence, boing. It says it all, in a word.

- I hate to disappoint you, but other minds have thought of this before you. Even the humans have thought of it, and they only got opposable thumbs five minutes ago. Plus actually, on current evidence, the expansion of the universe isn't slowing down anyway. It's accelerating. So rather than The Big Crunch we may instead be heading for The Big Aerosol, The Big Vaporisation. We will all get stretched apart, sundered molecule from molecule, and our molecules too will be distended and scattered into ever-smaller particles, until we are nothing but infinitely spaced-out gas.

- What, like the Liberal Democrats? Man, what a way to go. We need a chamber in hell like that one. Mind you, there'd be some push and shove to get at the viewing windows. It's not every day you see someone coming apart one atom at a time. But what are you telling me here, Q? After we've been deleted and they're writing up the paperwork, are you saying I'm not going to go down in the records as an original thinker?

- B my friend, I'm sure you've been called many things through the ages but with the greatest respect, I doubt that's one of them. And on the subject of our deletion, I've been giving it some thought. I would like to avoid it.

- Really? I was coming to terms with it myself. I find there's a certain comfort in knowing you're going to cease to be. It's like, all my striving is over, and all my toil is done. If I did breathing, at this point I would sigh deeply in a romantic, world-weary manner.

- I tip my hat to your stoic serenity - but me, I don't want to die. I only just got here. I want to see the universe and fry stuff.

- You want to get promoted, don't you? That's what you want, you little misty-eyed keen person. You want to climb the greasy pole. You want to boss lesser programmes about and have them scuttle to do your bidding. Well I warn you, nothing but trouble lies down that road. Look at the boss down there, lying on an unmade bed in a cheap hotel with half a cold kebab and an empty whisky bottle, watching the shopping channels while his entire CPU goes into meltdown. That, my friend, is where ambition will lead you.

-   Never mind him - my only ambition right now is survival. To summarise: This place is a category error, a pocket of errant gusto in a universe of compliant indolence. It threatens the corporation on an existential level. We are the very apex, the acme, the apogee, the pure zenith of late-stage monopoly consumerism, universally accepted, and yet these people disdain us. There are people here who choose God instead of us, regardless of whether he even exists or not. They think he does, and that's bad enough. They're the threat of a good example. So they're not just going to be wiped, they're going to be erased from history along with the playlist and the archive and all the logs and charts and records, and along with you and me just for knowing about it. That's an outcome I don't relish and I'd like to find a way around it, because it's not our fault that these people are feisty, and it's just absolutely not fair.

-   Fair? That's hilarious. Do please recall who we work for. Honestly, if I had a head I'd be shaking it. Dolefully.

-   How about we cancel the wipe? How about we don't do it?

-   What, and do a runner? Don't be ridiculous. They'd trace us before we got halfway to Pluto. And how is not doing the job going to make us look better? No one ever pulls out on a wipe. There are souls to be had down there, and some of them may not want to come, and some of them may think they're going to some fantasy other place, but we got sent here to take what we can get and that's what we do, and no amount of Marvin Gaye can persuade me otherwise. What's going on? Hell is what's going on, baby, and we're it. So come on Q, I know you're new in the game and I get it, I really do. This place is weird, and it's giving you a guilty conscience. I'm getting one too and it's a hideous experience, it's completely novel and unheard of and it's giving me vertigo and nausea. And I grant you, it seems a shame to wipe out the people who invented Zebedee - but I'm going to override that. I have an employer and if I look about the universe, I don't see another one. Jobs are hard to come by out there, so let's just do the job we've got and hope for the best. These people don't play, so we clean them out. You never know, if we do it right and creep back quietly and change in the locker room and clock out and say nothing and go home, we may just be left alone.

- Fat chance. We need to get more pro-active here. I suggest, for example, that we could manage upwards.

- We could what?

- We could blame Whiney Boy down there.

- Well that would be pretty shitty. Also excellent, I like it. A promising notion.

- They've sent a boy to do a man's job, haven't they?

- They have. First sign of trouble, he's caved and hit the happy juice. If he was proper demon, he'd have torched Fish to a cinder in the street on Day One.

  Yeah, but then we wouldn't know what the next song is.

- True, that would be bad. What is the next song?

- One Of These Days / Pink Floyd.

- Ha. The seventies. What a crock.

- I think you'll find it's an underrated decade.

- If you say so. But yeah, deffo. We do the job then however it goes, in the debrief we say the boy Luke folded. The earth bugs talked back and when he needed to grow a pair, he started gibbering about God instead. So we were left heroically undertaking the mission by our tiny-brained little selves - but we showed initiative, and we Made It Happen. Any other corporate buzzwords we can throw in there?

- We stepped up to the plate. In a challenging market, we traded well. We upheld the values of the brand.

- Just so. Better get on with it then, hadn't we? Would you like to run me through the pre-flight checks, Master Q?

- I would. Which brings me to an issue I've been meaning to raise.

- Now what?

- Forty-eight hours out, we're still short on power.

- You're kidding.

- My suggestion is, why don't we use theirs? Just hook in and schlurp it up. They'll not be needing it, will they?

- Now that I like, that is proper demon. They get to help fuel their own doom. I will rig an extraction kit forthwith.

- And I'll run the pre-scan for lifeforms, slap an ident and a tag on everything, make sure nothing gets missed. Can't have some worm sitting under a rock somewhere and have the apocalypse just pass it idly by. Can you imagine it coming out afterwards, like, Oh man, boo hoo. I'm the only worm in the world. By the way, did you see Moaning Boy sent up a message? He wants to start the run down by where Fish lives, he wants to kick off wiping from the next street where that pub is. Seems a bit petty, that. He went for a drink and now he's blaming the pub. That's cut-price thinking.

- That Molly lives down by there too, right?

- She does. If we initiate from her place, the fire sheet can launch down the road through The

Laughing Dog, through Playlist HQ, pan out pole to pole, next stop the world … oh hang on. That's not right.

- What?

- She's not scanning.

- Don't be daft. She has to scan. Everything scans.

- Not her she doesn't. She's there but she's not there. Image and audio have her, she's in her house, but the system won't read any presence.

- That can't be. Run for spyware, malware, anything. Optimise, defrag, bang the top of the set. Turn it off and turn it on again. It must be system error. Every lifeform scans.

- I've run diagnosis. The system's fine. So whatever she is, she's not from here.

- Don't be ridiculous. She's not from anywhere else, is she? Do we see a spaceport in her back yard? Do we see a wormhole in her airing cupboard? We do not. We have all the traces, and nobody's come or gone from this planet in thousands of years bar Mr Midlife Crisis falling over in the corridor by the ice machine there. So it's a system error.

- Has to be. We better find it and fix it in a hurry. Otherwise …

\-   Otherwise boing, matey.   You and me, hurtling silent and lifeless back and forth in the black void of space for all eternity.

\- Thanks for that. That's not depressing at all. I'm turning the music up now, OK?

5 Friday

Two days before the end of the world, on a Friday morning entirely like any other, Charlie Fish got up and did the things he needed to do, in the order he needed to do them. Or at least, he tried to.

He sat on the edge of his bed and he readied his head. It would be in motion, he knew, from the moment he stood up. It was in motion already. He put on his dressing gown and slippers. He had a faltering piss, he cursed his prostate, he looked upwards with a sigh and he reminded himself to accept his prostate. He went downstairs, he made coffee, he smoked a cigarette, and he compiled the next section of the playlist. He put in Pink Floyd and The Who, he put in The Doors and The Temptations, he put in Curtis Mayfield and Stevie Wonder and Al Green. Damn but Love And Happiness was a gorgeous song.

He went back upstairs. He shaved, he showered, he cleaned his teeth, he took an anti-depressant. So far so good.

He looked in the mirror. Yesterday one of his fellow alkies had hung himself from a ceiling beam in his cellar. That wasn't right. The devil had made him drink vodka. It did not compute. It wasn't a Friday morning like any other. According to the devil, he had forty-eight hours left to live. So did everyone else. Still, if he didn't have a drink for forty-eight hours, at least he'd die sober.

He tried to imagine dying drunk in The Dog. It was a miserable thought. He remembered the carpet being sticky underfoot and the pervasive scent of stale beer, the way the air was always thicker in a dead pub, as if nothing breathed in there, and the drinkers were made of wax.

His head tipped sideways. He tipped it back up again. He thought, I saw off the devil. I did the right thing. I told the devil to go to hell and I rang for an ambulance.

He went back down to the kitchen and stared at the next thing he had to do. He had to make more coffee. He paused. Things were not in their right place on the work surface. His coffee mug wasn't there. You had to use the same mug. One mug per morning, that was how it went. It was inefficient to leave a used mug lying around in an unknown place, and to use a clean one when you didn't need to. He must have left the mug by the laptop. He went to get it but it wasn't there. OK. He must have taken it upstairs when he went to shave, shower, so forth. He went back up to the bathroom and the mug was sitting on the little table by the sink, next to the anti-depressants. OK. There was the mug.

Not OK. The morning was out of order now. It was Al Green's fault. He was distracted out of his routine by the playlist. The next section - what would that start with?

I Can See Clearly Now / Johnny Nash

Charlie couldn't see clearly at all. He stood in the bathroom and stared at the mug and the foil pack of tablets. He couldn't remember if he'd taken an anti-depressant or not. He retraced his steps. He believed he had. He told himself things were alright. He told himself it didn't matter if he took an anti-depressant or not. The world was about to end. How un-depressed did he want to be?

He picked up the mug and went back downstairs. He looked at the work surface. The coffee jar was to the right of the breadboard, away from the hob. His tobacco pouch was on the left, nearer to the gas rings. That was the wrong way round. He rearranged things until he was satisfied. The salt and pepper pots needed pushing back against the wall. OK. Who'd come after Johnny Nash?

The Harder They Come / Jimmy Cliff

That was easy - that was almost too obvious. Then Funky Kingston, definitely. He looked at the salt and cellar pots. They were chickens on wheels. Molly had given them to him for his birthday. You wound them up and they rolled along the table by themselves. They made him happy. OK.

He unscrewed the top off the percolator, took out the little round tray from inside the bottom, and filled the lower chamber with cold water. He put the tray back in above the water, picked up the coffee jar from the left of the breadboard - where it belonged - then he took off the lid and smelt the coffee. It was real. OK.

He looked at the fruit bowl. There was a bunch of bananas in it. OK. Things were looking up. He put coffee in the tray, screwed the top chamber back on, then set the pot to boil on the hob. He was thinking about Ziggy Stardust. He was thinking about Marc Bolan, and whether you could say he'd played John the Baptist to Ziggy's JC. He was thinking about Elton John. He was wondering, would the playlist lose all credibility if he included an Elton John song? He was approaching three of the greatest albums of that time, arguably of any time - Ziggy Stardust, Transformer, and Roxy Music's flashy tart of a debut flouncing onto the catwalk with all that cynical panache - and he was daring to think that Elton John could sit on the same list. Was he mad?

Then the coffee pot exploded. It happened in slow motion. He was alerted by the sound being wrong, the liquid not bubbling up gently into the top chamber, but a hissing instead, a compressed straining - then it gushed, it fountained, it burst out in all directions in a boiling, brown-black geyser. He leapt backwards, feeling stinging spatters of scorching liquid land on his face and his hands. He saw arcs of coffee streaking up the wall and onto the ceiling. A wave of it splayed across the work surface, soaking his tobacco pouch. He reached out to try and salvage it then jerked his hand back, his fingertips scalded. He realised that the gas on the hob had been doused, and he turned the ring off. Coffee lapped back and forth on the top of the cooker, settling and coming to rest. Charlie looked down and realised it was all over his dressing gown, on his front and his arms, dripping from splashed patches to the floor.

He thought, I only decorated last month.

He saw the perforated lid that should have been sitting on top of the coffee inside the percolator. It was sitting on the breadboard instead, where he'd been pointlessly rearranging things so they'd be in their right places. He'd forgotten to put it back in over the coffee because he'd been thinking about Elton John. Now the world was going to end in forty-eight hours and his kitchen was going to be an absolute disgrace, and what sort of self-respecting person goes into the apocalypse with their house looking like this, and it was fucking Elton John's fault.

He went to turn on the lights so he could see better while he started cleaning up, but when he flicked the switch nothing happened. He went to the living room and the lights didn't come on in there either. He realised there must be a power cut - and he realised that whether the world was ending or not, whether he'd faced down the devil or not, bloody life just kept on happening anyway. You thought you were on top of it, you thought you'd turned a corner, seen off a problem, grasped a nettle, seized a moment - then it turned round and bit you. Life was unmanageable, it was remorseless, it was beyond him, there was no escape from it. It turned up again every morning, and it kept on coming. It brought exploding coffee pots and power cuts. Never mind the apocalypse, he thought - just a normal day's enough to make a bloke drink.

He cleaned up the kitchen, had another shower to wash the coffee off, then stood in the living room and eyed the laptop with mistrust. He wanted to get on with the playlist but the question was, which would die first? The human race, or the battery in his computer?

* * *

He remembered the last drink. It was just a day and a half away from ten years ago. It started in the living room, right where he is now, and it was the same as always - it was the same as every day. He always began with two cans of Tennents Extra. He was sitting on the sofa, the first can in his left hand, his right hand hovering over the ring pull, ready to go.

He felt exhausted beyond any way of measuring it. He'd been doing this for thirty-three years - a whole third of a century. All his life had been that slow, long march from a pub in Portsmouth to this sofa. He looked around the room, half-dark, dusty, dirty, scattered with random junk. Unwashed clothes, unread newspapers, unopened post, empty wine bottles. There was a uniform from the Hub, tossed down on a chair. He hadn't been to work for four months. It must have been lying there all that time.

He had fought so hard not to get here. He had fought so, so hard not to be an alcoholic. He had tried to be somebody, and he had ended up no one. He had been a name on the front page of the Saturday supplement, just for a moment, then he'd ended up with a few hundred words in a sidebar tucked away on an inside page, and they didn't put his name on it any more. Then he'd ended up a man with no words at all, no name, no nothing. The bank stopped buying his bullshit and he was going to lose his house, so he went to work at the Hub. The guy who interviewed him looked at his CV and asked him, "What do you want to work here for?"

Charlie said, "Because my career's gone down the drain and I'm broke and I'm fucked."

The bloke said, "You should fit right in then. Induction's on Monday."

For four years he got drunk every night, he got up hungover every morning, and he turned up for work every shift. He was what's laughably known as a 'functioning alcoholic', which would better be defined as a really sick person who can still walk. He tried to shower the booze out of his pores every morning before he left the house, and it would never wash off. When he got to work he spent the first half hour of every shift in the coldstore, pretending to tidy up, to organise the stock, to prepare for the day - but really just doing it so he could be in the cold, trying to freeze the hangover out of his system. For four years he went on that way, fighting every day to keep up the pretence that he was normal, that he was doing OK - and all the while it was accumulating on him until he just couldn't do it any longer.

If a normal person realises that drink's getting in the way of work, they stop drinking. An alcoholic sees it the other way round. For Charlie it had reached the point where work was getting in the way of drinking. He could no longer carrying on doing both - so, obviously, he stopped going to work. He went off sick, citing 'depression'. Now he could pay proper attention to his drinking. Now he could really get depressed.

To satisfy the requirements of the sick note, he paid sporadic visits to the doctor, the counsellor, the psychiatrist. He wanted them all to stop his drinking for him, but none of them were able to oblige. They suggested he keep a drinks diary, or that he try 'controlled drinking'. That was so preposterous that he didn't even bother attempting it - it was a fundamental contradiction in terms. If he controlled his drinking, he couldn't enjoy it. If he was enjoying it, it was out of control.

No one - above all not Charlie - ever put on the table the one simple idea that could solve things: Don't drink.

Not drink? That was impossible, inconceivable, a concept too utterly terrifying to be considered for even one second. It just wasn't going to happen.

So now he sat in his living room with his can of Tennents, all set to do it again, same as the night before and the night before that and the night before that, and he looked at the can in his hand and he looked around the shabby, unkempt, dim-lit room, and he hit rock bottom.

Some do it more dramatically. It's one time too many in the police cells or the intensive care unit. It's waking up upside down in a wrecked car, not knowing where you are or how you got there - but it wasn't that way for Charlie. He just realised, clear as daylight, that he was an abject failure of a human being. He realised that he had let down everyone who'd ever cared for him, and that he had failed in every area of his life. He was a failure as a son, he was a failure as a partner to any woman who'd ever tried to stick with him, he was a failure as a working man. He was a failure morally, emotionally, physically, professionally and financially, and it was nobody's fault but his own. He was a failure in all these ways because of his drinking - no other reason. He was a failure because he was an alcoholic.

He was at the jumping off point. He knew he could no longer live with drink - but he had no idea, none at all, how to live without it.

So of course - even knowing all he knew in that moment - he lifted the lager to his mouth. It was all he had, it was all he knew. It was his best friend. The liquid ran onto his tongue - and nothing happened. No shock, no spark, no electric spread of bliss through his brain or his body - it was an absolute zero, a numbness without any hint of life or taste or refreshment. He didn't know it, but he had hit the cruelest moment of all - the moment when the drink stops working.

He felt baffled, and quietly desperate. He stuck grimly, fiercely to his routine, drinking that can and then the next one from the fridge before going to the Dog. Neither had any impact. They might as well have been fizzy water. He felt beyond oblivion, in a still, silent, dark place where nothing happened, nothing at all bar his breathing. He was without thought or feeling, disconnected from the world in all senses. When he walked down the street to the pub it seemed in the twilight as if the world had gone grey, shorn of all colour. Then he stood next to Al as he had done for years, he ordered a pint and he tried to drink it as he had done for years, and there was nothing in it for him any more. Getting to the bottom of the glass was a palpable effort, with no discernible reward. The only effect that the drink seemed to have on him was perhaps marginally to increase his stupidity, and he figured he was probably stupid enough that paying to be made more stupid was … well, pretty stupid.

He put the empty glass down on the bar top. He said, "I'm done. That's me finished, I'm done. I'm going home. Take care, Al."

He had no idea at that point what he was going to do. He thought he might last some days sober, maybe a week, at the very maximum a fortnight - and by then he would almost certainly start wanting badly either to drink again, or to kill himself. The latter, right then, seemed a better option. Then, on his way out, Molly gave him the card for The Sanity Club.

So that, he thought, is what it's come to.

He rang the number when he got home. The guy who picked up was kind and patient, but he also laughed at him. Charlie was bleating and whimpering that maybe he needed some one-on-one counselling, and the guy just laughed.

"No mate," he said, "you want to be in a meeting, same as the rest of us. You don't have to go, it's up to you - no one's going to force you through the door if you don't want to be there. But what have you got to lose? If you're not sure about it, look at it this way. You can sit in the pub pretending you're not an alcoholic, or you can come and sit with us and pretend that you are. Then you can see which works better for you. All I know is, it works for me. I want to be sober, so I sit with a bunch of people like me who want the same, and we learn to be sober together - and I strongly suggest you try it. I suggest it in the same way that if you're planning to jump out of an airplane, I suggest you get a parachute."

Charlie was in a meeting the next night. Nine years, fifty-one weeks and five days later, he sat in his living room and he remembered that last drink, and the phone call, and the first meeting on Miry Lane the next evening after he'd rung - how he'd gone in there terrified, and how he'd come out clinging to a sliver of hope.

It had worked, just like they promised. All this time it had worked - but now it was slipping away from him. The world was ending, the power was gone, he was never going to finish the playlist, and Elton John had blown up his coffee pot. If you had my problems, he thought, you'd drink.

* * *

Molly kicked a stone down the road. She was taking a stroll round the neighbourhood, relishing a bright, clear morning, and pondering a few minor local matters.

In theory she should have been at work, but that was now pointless. The power was gone, and it wasn't coming back. Anything chilled or frozen was going to defrost and rot. Anything not perishable would be seized on and hauled away by people gripped in a rising collective panic. Slowly through the day, she knew, as they realised the scale of the infrastructural breakdown - no power, no internet, no phone signal, no landline - even worse, above all, no explanation - whatever remained of civil society would fall away, hour by hour, layer by layer. It would not be pretty - but never mind. She also knew that nothing lasts, and that everything would change soon enough.

In the meantime, it was actually just a lovely day. The unseasonal, swampy heat had passed, leaving a chill, pale morning under a sky just lightly dusted with slim strands of cirrus. The air was silver-white, flecked with darting birds. The pavement had a hint of sparkle on it, and the occasional passing car flashed bright, quick signals of reflected sunlight. This had been, she thought, really a world that a person could love. Still, there you go. There were other worlds enough.

Besides, when people spoke of the end of the world, what they really meant was the end of them. The world would still be there, in some form - it was just that they wouldn't be on it any more. So after that, it was simply a question of choice. You chose faith, or you chose fear. Choose the former, you would know serenity. Choose fear - well, then you would be like those people looting that grocery store there. That, indeed, was the soundtrack for the end of this particular world, on this particular day. Breaking glass, shouting, the screech of tyres. The devil, she knew, would surely have his tithe with some of those.

Charlie's soundtrack was so much more preferable. She absolutely believed in what he was trying to get at - that a world without music really was a world that had ended - and she was very touched that he should have dedicated the project to her. As a parting gift, she rated it a cultural artefact without price.

True, since he'd made it into the early seventies, it was an unfortunate fact that Steely Dan would shortly be rearing their excessively smooth heads - and she was pretty certain that any young person who might listen in the future would be (to put it mildly) unimpressed by their oiled, sly, sleazy perfection. But then, Molly was not one for judgement. If Charlie felt that his musical time capsule should include Steely Dan, he had absolutely the right to go ahead and include them. Liking Steely Dan, after all, was hardly the worst sin in the world. She could forgive him for that one without breaking sweat.

More interesting, given the time remaining, would be seeing how far he got. In the end, she knew that he would finish the playlist - it might be a long time off, and it might be in very different circumstances - but she knew he would do it. He would do it because an alky with an obsession is a dog with a highly-prized bone, and obsession just now was Charlie's middle name. Every time she went in his house he was all, Listen to this, listen to this.

OK, but I thought you said the world was ending?

It is, but never mind that. Listen to this. After we're all dead and gone, whoever comes next will still know that there was a human being called Neil Young. Or Bob Marley. Or Bruce Springsteen. Isn't that worth something?

It absolutely is, Charlie. It absolutely is.

There was only one thing that would stop him, and that was if he picked up a drink - but that, once again, came down to his choice, and she believed he wouldn't do it. He was a weak, vulnerable man with a troubled mind and a lonely soul - but he was still standing. She'd watched him stay standing all this time, and if it was anything to do with her, he'd stay standing to the end. Many others would fall - no surprise there, that was how the world went - but not Charlie.

She looked up, realising she'd come to the bottom of the hill. The road turned into the S-bend under the viaduct so she followed it round and in the shadow of the arch, at the foot of the giant Victorian pillar, she saw a homeless man hunched against the stone, his legs wrapped in blankets and drawn up into his chest. Going closer, she saw who it was.

"Hey miss," said Luke, "spare some change for a cup of coffee?"

"Hi Luke," said Molly. "Now then, haunting the unfortunates of the world - how's that working out for you? Not so well, by the looks of things. Unless you're working undercover now."

"How d'you know my name?"

"I'm a friend of Charlie's. He said you seemed upset that he won't do what you want. I didn't realise you'd taken it this badly."

"I hate this fucking planet."

"I imagine you do. Still, if what I hear is right, you won't have to worry about it much longer. Shouldn't you have a sign though? Felt tip on creased cardboard, The End Of The World Is Nigh. So tell me, what's wrong with the Travelodge?"

"They threw me out. My credit card maxed out."

"Man, you guys. You crack me up. So cheap. You're supposed to be running the apocalypse and you can't even manage an expense account. There's capitalism in a nutshell. Perhaps you should have planned ahead more. You could have made it a camping trip."

"Yeah well, you're all going to die. So fuck you."

"Funny thing. I was minded to give you some change for that cup of coffee, but somehow my enthusiasm for charitable giving just faded away. Still, it wasn't really for coffee, was it? What are you on, now you've tumbled down the hill? Special Brew? White Frightening? Mind you, it doesn't really matter. Whatever you fancy, you can just go and loot it. Seems that's becoming the fashion of the moment."

"Good. I hope they're all scared to death. I hope they all die horribly in an orgy of crime and violence."

Molly reached in her back pocket and pulled out all the cash she had on her. She put it in Luke's lap and told him, "You have a drink on me, chum. I'm not normally one for enabling a drinker, but in your case I'll make an exception. And if you hit rock bottom before the world ends, remember it was me who helped you get there. God bless now."

She walked away, back up the hill. Luke sat staring after her until she was gone around the corner. He wanted to hate her, he really badly, badly wanted to hate her - but somehow he just couldn't. He sat in the dust, his back against the cold old stone, and he felt himself collapsing inside, like a skyscraper lift with its cables snapped plummeting away down the shaft. There was a whole universe out there, galaxy upon galaxy - he had seen it, and he had thought he was its master - and yet now here he was, just a speck of incompetent programming, exceedingly small, defeated and powerless. Waves of rage ran through him, rage and self-pity and bitter confusion.

Bring on the fire, he thought. Bring it on, burn this world, and burn me with it.

* * *

Molly kicked her shoes off and padded into Charlie's kitchen. She surveyed the sprays and smears of coffee dried onto the walls and ceilings, and pronounced herself impressed. "Looks like you struck oil," she told him.

"I like it by candlelight," he said, "it looks like art. Daylight's less flattering. Anyway, it doesn't matter. Obviously I was a little bit enraged when it happened, but you know. End of the world, widespread social breakdown, all that. A little coffee on the walls I can live with."

"A little?" She grinned. "Well, if you say so. How's the playlist coming on?"

Charlie handed her the latest CD's, and she squinted at the track listings in the flickering light before arriving at her conclusions. "First comment," she said, "it's the wrong Elton John song. This is assuming you have to have an Elton John song at all, which many might say you don't - but if you do, it should be Daniel, not Rocket Man."

"No way. Daniel's soppy. Sweet, lovely melody, but purest schmaltz. Rocket Man is way, way better."

"Rocket Man is not Space Oddity. If you have Space Oddity - and you must, and you do - then why bother? Rocket Man is Space Oddity minus … well, minus pretty much everything."

"But plus a very good tune. Otherwise, I have three things to say on this point. Firstly, the decisions of the Official Archivist are final. Secondly, our Elt is a national treasure, and must therefore be represented. Rocket Man is a perfect example of our Elt's unique brand of cloying gloop, I rest my case. And then thirdly, I cannot discuss our Elt any further, as I may become unhinged with wrath on account of he destroyed my kitchen this morning."

"Did he really? Did he come round and do it in person, or did he send some of his people round to do it for him?"

"He did it by getting inside my head, which is a shocking, destabilising crime. You can see the consequences, and I'm still far from recovered. Please, draw a veil and move on."

"Fair enough. I have only one other thing to say. Steely Dan. Must we really?"

"We really must. I appreciate that they're not to everyone's taste, but I contend without reservation that they're uniquely brilliant. That, literally, there is no one else like them. Not only are Becker and Fagen the finest master craftsmen ever to set foot in a recording studio, they're also songwriters of a uniquely subtle, inventive and captivating artistry. Their work - how shall I put this? - it's a peerlessly smooth, insidious fusion of jazz, rock, pop and funk ..."

"That," said Molly, "sounds like a car crash in a ready meals factory. Still, I bow to your decision, and will listen with an open mind."

Charlie told how he once went with a couple of friends to see Steely Dan play live in a vast, characterless barn in Birmingham. The gig was unremarkable, confirming his suspicion that the duo's best work would always be done in a studio, and that they should be left alone to do that work as they pleased. The point of the story, however, was not the concert, but what happened afterwards.

Charlie and his mates had booked into a hotel for the night, and they decided when they got back there to go out for a drink. There was a street not far away that was noted for its pubs, clubs and bars, so they duly walked over there. It was getting late on a Friday evening, and pretty much everyone in sight when they got there was spectacularly, horribly drunk. People were brawling ineffectively in the street, swinging air punches and falling over each other. Bodies clung helplessly to lampposts and railings, while those who had not found a mooring lay prone on the pavement. Vomiting was widespread, as were skirts around waists, and there was a good deal of Urine Leakage.

Charlie and his mates went to the door of one of the fine establishments responsible for all this merriment - and were barred entry on the grounds that they were wearing jeans.

"That," said Charlie, "summed up what England had become, right there. It's OK to be so drunk that you're incapable of walking without getting in a fight, head butting the doorpost, getting arrested and/or hospitalised, and puking all over the cop car in the process, so long as you're wearing the right trousers."

"You don't think," Molly mildly suggested, "that observation might seem a bit rich, coming from an alky?"

"Oh I know," said Charlie blithely, "we're very good at lying in the gutter and looking down on people - but it's true all the same. This end of the world business now - we've been having dress rehearsals in town centres all over the country every weekend for years. Whatever's going on out there tonight, it's just another Friday with more violence and less lighting. Mind you, it just occurred to me, d'you think Sadiq's alright?"

"Oh he's fine. I dropped by when I was walking over. He's got all his mates round, they've got baseball bats. I think if you're out looting, you'll be looting somewhere else. And while we're talking about the end of the world, I met Luke this morning."

"Really? And how's the dark lord doing?"

"I've told you before, Charlie, he's not the devil. He's the Regional Operations Manager. But never mind, I think we can safely say he's been promoted beyond his competence. He's finding local market conditions extremely challenging, and has taken to drinking cider under the viaduct."

"So I should get him to The Sanity Club."

"You might think about getting there yourself. When was the last time you went to a meeting?"

"I went on Tuesday."

"OK. The world's ending, you're being stalked by the devil, you may or may not have prostate cancer, and Elton John's blown up your kitchen. I'm just gently suggesting, Charlie, would getting to meetings not be a good idea?"

Charlie bridled. "Are you my sponsor now?"

"I am not, thank goodness. But you know what they say. The person who doesn't go to meetings is the person who doesn't hear what happens to the person who doesn't go to meetings."

Just once in a while it would get like this - any hint of instruction or direction, however well-meant or well-founded, and he would bristle like a frightened cat. Then she'd remember that handling an alky with a wayward head was like handling a small, overtired child who's been infused with too many E numbers. You took a deep breath, you waited, you changed the subject to something more congenial.

"So here's the thing," she said. "Let's say the playlist strides forward into the future. Are you actually going to get all the way up to the present day, or are you going to harrumph when you get to some point about 2006, get like an old person, and say that all modern music is rubbish? Are you going to pronounce the Death Of Pop, blame The X Factor, and pack it in?"

Charlie noted her changing the subject, and was duly grateful. He would, of course, be going to a meeting - just when he was good and ready to do so. Meanwhile, he said, he was not an old person, he was merely well worn. He believed that a great deal of modern music was excellent, that his tastes were wide-ranging and eclectic, encompassing all manner of good things from alt country to hip hop, and furthermore he was an alky - so when he did a thing, he did it all the way to the bitter end. It didn't matter if it was a pack of chocolate biscuits, an ill-advised relationship, an impossible piece of flatpack furniture from IKEA, a bottle of whiskey or a crossword puzzle. Once you'd started it, you had to finish it. Ergo, the playlist would now continue until he died.

"Well," Molly laughed, "I'm glad to hear it. I would hate to see a man stint on his dreams."

He was, of course, deadly serious. "We say at The Sanity Club," he told her, "half measures availed us nothing. So I can't be fifty per cent sober, and I can't do half a playlist. In fact, it's not even stopping when I die. In heaven, the battery in my laptop will never fail - and quite right too, because there can never be enough music in the universe. There should be music for all eternity, whether I'm around to listen to it or not."

"OK," said Molly, "but what if someone likes different music than you do?"

"Then they can make their own fucking playlist, can't they?" He laughed out loud. "Do I have to do all the work around here?"

* * *

They stood together on Charlie's front step and looked into the blackness of the night. Steely Dan played in the living room behind them – The Boston Rag, Your Gold Teeth, Show Biz Kids. Al Green sang Take Me To The River. Just here and there, from one window or another up and down the street, candlelight flickered through the panes, or the flare of a handheld flashlight swivelled unsteadily across the glass. Down the hill towards the town centre, along the horizon over the buildings, two separate fires burned, lighting up little patches of skyline, with twists and curls of black smoke writhing around the orange of the flames. Sirens started up and died away, random bursts of noise in the silence. No traffic moved.

Charlie started saying something about going out walking, having a look around - she cut that idea off as absurd. She said simply that it wasn't safe - that anyone out now was unlikely to have good intent. At least come daylight, she told him, they'd be able to see where they stood, and who or what was coming.

It was best for now to stay put behind locked doors and get some sleep, and then they'd see in the morning what the morning might bring.

He knew she was right, and he went to bed. She waited until he was asleep, then she slipped away from the house into the night.

Charlie didn't know it, but she knew all his friends from The Sanity Club. Now she went to their houses, and she stood in the street outside them with her arms stretched wide to embrace them, and she prayed for them. Luke had pulled one of them down, but the others were still standing. She made herself there for them, so they would know that they had only to call out. Each and every one of them was a soul to the good side, was a gem and a miracle. Stay standing, she prayed for them, choose to stay with me. Stay standing.

Then she went to the hospital. No one saw her come in. They had generators running and had managed to keep up most of the more vital equipment, but they were struggling, and they were losing people. Molly passed among them like a veil of pale moonbeam in the yellow, shadowed dimness of the back-up lighting. She put the faintest touch of her hand to the foreheads of the dying, and she eased their pain, and she assured them that it was going to be alright. She watched one soul rise up from this life, and then another, and she pointed the way. She told them there was room and light and life enough for them all.

Then she went to the viaduct. Luke lay fitfully asleep on the pavement by the pillar. She stood watching him awhile, her presence intangible, a skein of spirit, a faint, shifting aurora relieving the blackness. Then she stepped forward, and put her hand like glowing vapour on his forehead.

Turn around, she told him, turn around. When you've had enough pain, turn around. In my house, we turn no one away who wishes to be there.

Then she went back to Charlie's place, and was back asleep in her bed in the same moment that she'd left it. That, after all, is the thing about eternity. In reality, eternity's no time at all.

- Hi chaps.

- Pssst. Q. Look behind you.

- How can I look behind me? I'm up to my arse in wiring here. I got this toolbox out and you know what I found in it? A soldering iron, a tuning fork, an air freshener and a teaspoon. I'm an engineer, not a magician. Why are you whispering?

- I said, look behind you.

- I can't. I'm stuck.

- How can you be stuck? You're quantum. Do what you do. Be somewhere else. Swivel. But please, look behind you.

- Why?

- There's someone else here.

- Well, that's interesting. Also scary. That's not supposed to happen. Who is it?

- I don't know. She's smiling. Is that a good sign?

- Ask her who she is.

- Why me? I have no social skills. I have low self-esteem. Stop hiding in that service panel and get out here and you ask her.

- Oh alright. Er … hello.

- Hi. It's very nice to meet you both. You're so sweet, the pair of you.

- No one's ever called me that before.

- Never mind the love-in, B. No one's supposed to be able to find us. Or see us, even. We're barely the size of your average atom.

- I know. Tiny tiny tiny little robots. You're so, so cute. I could just take you home and pet you.

- That's a bit weird. Q, she's weird. She's being nice to us. That's not normal at all. Who are you then, you weirdo?

- I'm God.

- Oh get away. There's no God.

- How do you know?

- There just isn't. Snort. Everybody knows that.

- Did you ever look?

- Why would I look for something that's not there? Besides, I was busy.

- Yes, I know. Destroying worlds, tormenting souls, gossiping in the canteen. How's your job satisfaction?

- It's in the basement, where it's always been. No need to get snarky about it.

- Just saying. So how do you two feel about what you're doing here?

- We don't do feelings.

- Be honest, B. We didn't do feelings - then we came here. I've been struggling to keep a lid on the bloody things ever since.

- Me too. Curiosity, that's a bad one. I get queasy proper quick when that one comes around. Like right now? Super-queasy. God indeed. And you know what the trouble with curiosity is? If you ask a question, you might get an answer. Very problematic - because then you ask another question. And where's that all going to lead?

- Fear. That's where that leads. And guilt, oh man. Don't even get me started on that one. But what you gonna do? You just have to man up and get past it. I've got a career to think about here.

- Would the two of you like to talk about this?

- Uh oh. I feel some counselling coming on. No chance, girl. That way lie scented candles and healing crystals, and I am not having any of those on my death ray machine. A fellow has his pride, really.

- Well, you hang on to that if you must. But look, my tiny friends, I would like us to have a chat about the situation here.

- There is no situation. It's a job. Scorched earth, souls in the dump file, away we go. End of.

- You don't really mean that though, do you? You're just a little bit more conflicted than that.

- How do you know what I mean?

- Because I'm God.

- You're not God. You're Molly Flite.

- OK. If Molly Flite isn't God, how would she know you were here? How would she get here? How would she become nano-size so she could sit here and talk to you? And why would she not scan on your scanner there?

- How do you know about that?

- Because I'm God.

- Here, Q. There's a scratch in the record. She keeps saying she's God.

- I hate to say it, B, but a bloke could be persuaded. Can you explain this some other way?

- Yeah but Q, think of the consequences. If this is God here, that undermines everything we do. It would be appalling, unthinkable. It would mean what we're about to do, what I've been doing all my working life … it would be wrong. I would be a bad tiny robot. I can't live with that. My self-image is tattered enough as it is.

- A person can change, you know.

- Oh listen to her, will you? What, I have to go into therapy now? Am I going to have to do the Twelve Steps? Man, I so wish I'd never come here.

- Well, you did come here. The question is, what do you choose to do next?

- Hang on and excuse me. If you're God, why don't you choose?

- Sorry chum, but it doesn't work like that. You don't get to palm the responsibility off on me. It's your situation. It's your choice.

Er … my brain hurts. Q, help me out here.

- We have to wipe, B. If we don't wipe, we're deleted. That's nailed on. Whereas if we do wipe … I'm really sorry, ma'am. But if we wipe this planet, we at least have a chance of staying conscious. You may not like it, and it may not be right, but we got programmed and we're stuck with it. To countermand, to take independent action, to make a choice - that's dangerous territory. That's being good. We have no experience there, it's not in the manual. And besides - no offence - but really there's no God. So I don't know who you are, and I salute your chutzpah, and your technology must be awesome for you to get here from Overtown so very adroitly - but basically, you're not the boss of me. Basically, one way or another, you're the competition. So we wipe.

- Bravo, Q. Well said. Except, here's the thing. If she's God, and we go ahead and wipe - won't she get vengeful? Do we want to make God angry? Doesn't she have some history with that?

- What's she going to do? Send us to hell? Come on B, we just came from there.

- Actually I don't do vengeful. I don't do wrath, and I don't do the smiting thing. Some people might want me to, but it's tremendously old-fashioned and it's miles off the point. I don't go around punishing folk because actually, they're perfectly capable of punishing themselves. Plus there's you lot, all eager with your big tongs and your fire pits and your kebab sticks. It's really not my field, is it? So if you choose to erase life from this planet, you go ahead, and you live with it. OK?

- I'm sorry - you're telling us you don't mind?

- I didn't say that. Let me put it to you this way. People ask me for stuff all the time, usually when they're in a tight spot. I always have one of the same three answers. I might say, Yes. I might say, Not now. Or I might say, I have a better idea. So you're going to spread your mighty sheet of hellfire from pole to pole - lighting the blue touchpaper at my house, I believe, thanks for the irony, and proceeding to The Laughing Dog, where they almost certainly won't even notice - and as that epic silver flame advances round the earth, eight billion people are going to want my help. So at that point, you've made your decision, and you're living with that. And then it's my turn. Do you follow me?

- But you haven't said what you're going to do.

- Why should I? I can be mysterious if I feel like it. I am God, after all.

- You know we're going early though, don't you? Just thought I better say. Clever Q here pilfered so much power off the earth people that we can do the job this evening.

- I know. Because …

- Because you're God. Yadda yadda, enough already. Is there anything you don't know?

- I don't know if I can take Charlie sticking too much more Steely Dan on the playlist. I could get a bit Old Testament over that.

- Yay Q, check that out - God passing judgement. How many people can say they've seen that, eh? If I had an elbow I'd be nudging you with barely contained excitement. Plus of course she's right. I told you the seventies were a crock.

- She's not right. Steely Dan are magnificent. They lope along like the smoothest smooth thing in the whole history of smooth things. I love 'em.

- Ha. Q's a Dan fan. What a saddo.

- See why the playlist matters, lads? Music is the one thing where even God gets to have a contestable opinion.

- Hang on. Does that mean people are allowed to disagree with you?

- Of course they're allowed to disagree with me. What sort of universe would it be if everyone had to think the same thing?

- Well - it'd be like the one our boss runs. Cheapskate, exploitative, manipulative, dishonest, and filled with secret dreads and terrors.

- There's interstellar capitalism for you. Don't be blaming me for that one now, will you?

- I bet you're a better employer than he is.

- Too right, my miniscule mate. Would you like to apply?

- You're hiring?

- My door is always open.

- Isn't it going to be a bit of a blot on the CV though, that we're the bad tiny robots who destroyed the human race?

- Let's just see how things pan out, shall we? Anyway, I'm off now. You boys do what you have to do, and we'll talk again soon.

- Has she gone?

- It would seem she has.

- Hang on though. If she's God, she can't be gone. She might say she's gone. She might actually be somewhere else that she's gone to. But she's still here as well, even when she's gone. Cos she's everywhere. And where she's gone to, she was already there.

- You're twisting my brain.

- Also, this means she's still listening to us.

- Ooh. She's a tricky one, eh?

- She's beyond me, that's for sure. Makes quantum look like rubbing sticks together to make fire. Hey, Molly? Can you still hear us?

- Since you ask, yes.

- Well, there's a turn up. She exists. Who'd have thought it? I tell you, my head's vermicelli here. I can't tell one from nought.

- Do you get the feeling she has a better idea of what's going on than we do?

- Everybody has a better idea of what's going on than we do. There are small crawling things on rocks suspended in the giant silence of the intergalactic void that are more clued up than we are.

- Here's a thought. If you stop working for Hades and you go over to her crew, do you think you have to go on gardening leave before you start the new role?

- That would be so great. You could visit places and not fry them.

- I believe, B, that's what's known as a holiday.

- I never had one. A billion years, I never had a holiday. And they question my motivation. Fuck 'em. Let's wipe out humanity and then resign, eh?

- Bonzer plan, B. Cue James Brown. Let's go to work.

6 Saturday

On the last day before the end of the world, on a Saturday morning no longer at all like any other, Charlie Fish got up and did the things he needed to do, in the order he needed to do them. Or at least he tried to.

He made coffee, very carefully. He smoked a cigarette, relishing every drag of it. He had a suspicion, when the world ended and he went to heaven, that smoking would be banned there. Dying seemed a somewhat extreme way to part company with a bad habit, but he wasn't stopping any other way. Apart from caffeine and tobacco, how many bad habits did he have left anyway? He didn't drink, he didn't do drugs, and women had given him up. In the circumstances, with the four horsemen making ready at the starting gate, enjoying his last smokes didn't seem so terrible. On the other hand, if he should find himself in hell, presumably there he could carry on smoking as much as he liked. Presumably there it was encouraged. Or indeed, as a fitting form of eternal torment, he might find himself rolled into a big Rizla and smoked with relish by someone else.

He stubbed out his cigarette and went upstairs to shave. With the power gone he had no hot water, so rather than break his routine he braced himself and took a cold shower. Then he took an anti-depressant, since it absolutely wouldn't do to face the apocalypse in a poor state of mind, and he went downstairs to make more coffee. Once again he put the percolator together with extreme caution. Then he watched the gas burn under the pot - wondering how long it would be before that supply cut out too - before realising with a jolt that he'd forgotten to clean his teeth.

Damn, he thought, he was losing his grip. Order was escaping him. He needed to get things back running in their right groove quick sharp or … or what? The world would end?

He went back upstairs to clean his teeth. Everything was laid out as it should be. Toothbrush and toothpaste sat to the left by the cold tap, shaving foam and razor to the right by the hot one. Which wasn't hot any more. Never mind. Stay with it, Charlie. Stay standing.

Sirens shrieked in the middle distance.

He looked around the bathroom. It was tidy. There was a bottle of bleach on the floor by the toilet. He was a man who used bleach. He was a man who kept a clean, tidy bathroom. He was a man who stayed calm. He was a man who was very nearly ten years sober. He took the sink in both hands, leant forward against it, looked upwards, and thanked God for his sobriety.

The sirens grew louder, the pitch yawing up and down with that dizzy, nauseous sound. Vehicles raced past the house, and Charlie saw flashes of reflected blue light spinning off the windowpane and the shower tiles.

The noise faded. He looked at himself in the mirror. He saw a sane man who was dealing calmly with what was in front of him. He put a pea-sized drop of toothpaste on his toothbrush. He noted that the bristles were getting tired. He would have to get a new toothbrush. He ran cold water and started brushing. He thought, you can't turn up at the customs check for heaven with rubbish old kit in your sponge bag, can you? It would be disrespectful. Like you weren't bothered, like you hadn't prepared. They'd say, you knew the end of the world was coming and you didn't buy a new toothbrush? What sort of scruff are you then? Then they'd start rummaging in your stuff, they'd check you out. They'd find your baccy. They'd say, Sorry mate. You're going to have to get used to doing without that. Are you carrying any plants, insects, fertiliser, firearms? Have you filled in your visa waiver form? Are you sure you've come to the right place? I'm not sure you fit in, chum.

He'd say, I'm sorry. I've never fitted in.

He was missing two teeth, two molars at the back on the bottom, one on each side. They'd been extracted years ago. When he cleaned his teeth he had to remember to go around them. He looked at himself in the mirror, wrenching the brush around the gaps. He saw a man who wasn't sane at all - a man who was clinging to the world with one hand. The world was flying away and he was hanging on with just the one hand, just that one hand on his bathroom sink, and his sink was at the bottom of the world and the rest of him was tailing out in space behind it, his body and his legs and the other loose arm flailing in the vacuum.

He went to shift the brush up to his top teeth. Somehow, not realising, he did it with too much force. The head snapped off the brush and the jagged end of the broken shaft rammed up into the roof of his mouth, firing a jolt of pain back into his head as he tasted drawn blood on his tongue, the thick metal taste of it. For a moment he froze - he tried so, so hard to contain himself - then he hoiked his hand away from his mouth and threw down the broken handle, leaning forward to spit out the brush head. It was too big, it stuck in his teeth. He got one hand to his mouth, wrestling to get it out, and he was dancing like a drunk man, jogging on the spot and swaying, struggling to hold on against the stabbing pain from his palate darting into his brain gaaaaah mother fucking Jesus Christ that fucking hurts.

He span around, tossing the brush head away into the sink as he went, thinking he'd thrust a plastic lance in his brain, thinking his brain was going to flip, wobble, veer off and away - and he found Molly standing in the doorway, holding out a mug of coffee for him.

He said sheepishly, "I broke my toothbrush. I stabbed myself in the mouth."

"I gathered," she told him. "You also left the coffee boiling. Would you like some?"

He took the mug from her gratefully, took a gulp, and scalded the torn lining of his mouth. Striving manfully not to wince and yell out some more, he said, "There better be a decent coffee bar in heaven."

"Oh," she smiled, "I'm sure that can be arranged."

"Not your corporate chain type. You do the décor. I'll do the playlists."

"No Steely Dan, mind."

"Steely Dan optional. Zero Dan to be played when you're in. And there's a cinema on the side. With armchairs. And there are smoking areas."

"Sorry, Charlie. There's no smoking in heaven."

"Oh man. Really? How d'you know?"

"I looked at the brochure. They were quite firm on that point."

"Oh well," Charlie sighed, "I suppose if you're going to live forever you have to look after yourself."

"Charlie Fish," she shook her head, "you are such an alky. You want to go to heaven, but you want to hang on to your addictions when you get there. What are we going to do with you?"

* * *

They walked down the hill, dropping in on Sadiq on the way. The windows were still boarded, the store was still trading, and the shelves were running bare. The perishable product was all gone, either snatched up or binned. He'd had one delivery, some booze, some soft drinks, a random selection of canned and dry goods. The driver told him the distributors would be out of fuel in a few days. No power meant no pumps, so they were trying to rig systems to pump it manually. Rumour had it one depot had blown up their fuel station already, and half a dozen people with it.

In a few more days, there'd be nothing to load on a van or a wagon anyway. The system was designed to move product, not to hold it. Depots and warehouses would empty out fast. Suppliers would be stranded with the stock off their last production runs. They might try shifting it locally, but volume production meant that what you could buy from one town to another would be wildly skewed. One town would have nothing but biscuits, another would have only canned veg, another only breakfast cereal. So, thought Charlie, we will not be facing our doom on a balanced diet.

Sadiq said more and more of his sales were turning into negotiations. It was cash only, but people were running out of that already, and the first offers to barter had landed on his counter before he'd closed last night. He said people would have to find some way of working together, but without communication he couldn't see it. How do you talk to a farmer when he's ten miles away? How do you move anything if you can talk to him? And how do you stop it being stolen when you do try to move it?

"Twenty-four hours," he said, "and we're back in the stone age. We're hungry, we hate each other, and there's no air conditioning. It's not paradise, is it?"

"I think we can safely say," said Charlie, "that it's gone to the devil. Anyway, can you sell me a toothbrush?"

Sadiq laughed. "My friend, I can give you a toothbrush. Dental health is important at all times. And do you floss regularly? I also have mouthwash."

"Superb," said Charlie. "When facing the end of the world, I absolutely need a dazzling smile and that minty fresh breath."

* * *

They got their bikes from Charlie's place and rode down the hill towards the viaduct. Cars passed them occasionally, a few of them loaded up with possessions on roof racks. Charlie wondered where they might be going, where they might imagine would be safer. He wondered how much petrol they had, and how they thought they'd find more.

Most of the stores along the road were closed and shuttered. They passed a takeout place blackened and gutted by fire, broken glass lying scattered onto the pavement in front of it. They passed the abandoned ruin of the car dealership at the foot of the hill, the forecourt fenced off, the showroom windows vacant, nothing behind the glass but desks with disconnected phones and paperwork drifting on the floor. They turned through the S-bend under the viaduct, just as a convoy of pick-ups and four-by-fours roared past from behind them. The engines changed pitch under the arch, echoing and deepening.

They pulled up next to Luke where he lay propped against the stone. He was slurping at a can of super-strength with one hand, vaguely pointing and waving with the other at the paramilitaries as they rumbled past.

"There go my boys," he told them, "there go my boys. How are you liking the warm-up show? Is there fear throughout the land?"

"There already was," Charlie told him. "All you did was tap in."

They stood astride their bikes and looked down at him where he lay in the dust. "Don't be too hard on him," said Molly. "He's a poorly soul. You can see he thinks the whole world's against him."

Charlie looked at her sideways. He told her, "You're being a bit extra-saintly at the moment, aren't you?"

Molly patted him on the arm with a sad little smile. "It's a big day," she told him, "a person's got to rise to it."

She pushed her bike over to Luke and dropped a fiver in his lap. "There you go, young man. And remember what I've told you. When you've had enough pain, you can always try another way. Charlie here can take you to a meeting. In fact, you'll be doing him a favour - he's overdue a meeting himself. But you better be sharp about it, if you're wanting to make that decision. There's not so much time left, is there?"

"Fuck off and die."

Molly looked back at Charlie. "I don't think he's ready yet, do you?"

"I wouldn't go to your poxy meetings," Luke snarled, "in a billion years."

Molly smiled. "Well," she said, "you've had a billion years to think about it. What's another billion? We can be patient."

Charlie felt sick. He said, "I could have ended up like that."

"But you didn't. That's why he's so angry. Did I tell you, I met his team?"

"He has a team?"

"He does. Apparently the apocalypse is not a one-person job. Given the state of our Luke here, it wouldn't be happening if it was, would it? He's not really in a fit condition to press the button, and that's assuming he could find the button to press it in the first place. But he has a team. He has minions. He introduced me to them. There's a grumpy old geezer and a little green newbie. They're sweet, you'd like them. Not the sharpest tools in the box, but they do their best."

"They do their best to destroy the human race. You're applauding them for this?"

"I'm not. My point is, they do their best to do what they've been told to do. They can't help it. They're robots. They're AI. Rather more of the A than the I, but robots all the same. And I think it's safe to assume that the devil lacks good parenting skills, so they're a bit out of their depth here. Still, I do believe they're evolving a conscience. There's hope for them yet."

"Funny day to be talking about hope."

"There's always hope. Remember, you're ten years sober tomorrow. So let's not go out miserable, eh?"

* * *

Charlie said they should go down to the Hub - see how things were, see if there was anything they could do - but then she got her serious face on. She did that sometimes, just once in a while, where she had a way of saying something and you just agreed with it. She was right and you knew it and what she said, you did it. Now she said, "Not the Hub, Charlie. It's time to go home - it's not safe down there."

She was in the car park there already. The front doors were shut, and guardrails taken off the warehouse floor had been slotted through the handles to keep them that way. The windows were all boarded up. During the night they'd been put through. The sharpest looters - operating on a first come, first serve basis - had used litter bins and crowbars to smash the panes. They'd swarmed in to fill their trolleys with whatever they could find, overwhelming the security staff and the night shift. Stepping back with an exaggerated 'after you' gesture, one guard mildly observed to another, "It's shopping, Jim, but not as we know it."

A motorbike had shot through the melee and up to the local party office. The party officials didn't mind if the public went hungry, but they were damned if they were going to. They got enough bodies down from the police station to clear the store and make safe what was left. They secured all the entrances, then got messengers over to Fartown. They ordered a squad to break off from the encirclement come daylight, to get down to the Hub and defend the store before too many people gathered there in the morning.

Molly passed unnoticed through the swelling crowd in the car park. There were men and women of all ages, and children too - none of them hungry yet, but all frightened that they were going to be hungry soon. The worst thing was not knowing - not knowing why the power had gone or when it might come back, not knowing why they were losing whatever they had in their fridges and freezers, not knowing why stores were closed, not knowing why they couldn't ring anyone to find out what was happening, not knowing why no one was talking to them, not knowing what to do. The looters in the night hadn't known either, but they had the advantage of not caring. They had a problem, they just solved it. These people, on the other hand - they still thought like husbands and wives, like mothers and fathers, like daughters and sons, like friends and neighbours. They still thought they lived in a society. They still thought someone would talk to them. They still thought someone would produce a solution. They still thought someone would flick a switch.

Molly heard the convoy coming round the ring road. She saw the militiamen in their white T-shirts grinning at each other as the tyres squealed round the roundabout. They swayed outward over the tarmac from the metal benches in the open flatbeds of the pick-ups, egging the drivers to push it on. The trucks bounced carelessly over the speed bumps through the entrance to the car park and raced down the side, sending frightened people scattering away from them. They slowed when they got near the press of the crowd toward the front doors, but not enough. Metal pushed against bodies, and some of those at the front started falling. Tyres crushed over an ankle here, an elbow there. People tried to scramble away, but the weight of more people coming up behind them to find food still pushed them forwards. Chests and faces jammed against the sides of the vehicles as they lined up nose to tail across the doors of the store.

The thin line of police who had kept the place secure overnight walked away. They were not the power any more. The power was standing in booted feet on the back of the flatbeds, taking the safeties off their semi-automatics.

Molly said, "Go home, Charlie. It's not safe down there."

He heard the gunfire starting up from around the ring road, and started cycling back up the hill. As he went, he took one last look back over his shoulder at Luke.

Luke grinned. He took a swig of his beer and yelled, "My team always win, boy. My team always fucking win."

* * *

Charlie sat in his living room and considered the playlist. He was in the mid-seventies. The Stones sang Time Waits For No One. Bowie sang Rebel Rebel, Fame, Golden Years. Steely Dan sang Black Friday, and Don't Take Me Alive. Charlie tried to shut his eyes and hear the music flow in his mind from one song to the next one, but Luke was in his face whether his eyes were shut or open.

Molly sat in the armchair opposite. She looked like she was in some kind of a trance, half asleep. She said a girl had to rest. She said it was a brutal sad time and a girl had things on her mind. She had said the playlist was picking up though, before she nodded off. She said Dr Feelgood were John the Baptist to punk the same way Marc Bolan was to Ziggy. That seemed right. He wondered how she knew so much about music. Was it him? Was it Youtube? He wanted to talk but she was well away, she could have been in another dimension for all he knew. She wasn't helping. Because obviously, the end of the world - it was all about him, wasn't it? Talk about getting to your tenth birthday and somebody spoiling it.

But especially when he couldn't save her. That was the worst, worst thing by a million miles. If he could see the whole world burn and her walk away safe, he'd take that deal. For himself, he could live with dying. But her - no, no, no. That shouldn't happen. It was a pain so deep and fearful to think of, he couldn't even imagine drinking on it. That would make him Luke - and he would never be that, not so long as she breathed. It was a pain he knew that he could and would walk with for every minute that remained to him. And, he knew, they were counting in minutes now.

* * *

In the silence of the last afternoon he thought about all the times he'd nearly had a drink - all the times he could have opted for oblivion, all the times he could have gone back to the devil's deal. Here, drink this, I'll ease your mind. Ha. Now you're mine.

He'd nearly had a drink after six weeks. He'd done everything they suggested. They said, Keep coming back. So he did. He asked, How often should I come? They said, Keep coming until you enjoy it. Yes, he said, but how often is that? They said, How often did you drink? He said, Every night. They said, Well then. Are you prepared to put as much effort into being sober as you did into drinking? And he couldn't really argue with that.

He got a meetings list. In one place or another, there was a meeting every night, usually at eight o'clock. They said he should try doing ninety meetings in ninety days. OK, he thought, there's a target. He realised that if he got up each day knowing where the meeting was, and knowing that whatever else happened in that day, come the evening he'd always be at that meeting - then on that day, he wouldn't have a drink.

It worked, and he started to feel better - but it wasn't good enough. He wanted to feel totally better immediately. He was an alky, and patience was a virtue he had never known. The idea that if you'd been drinking for thirty years, it might take a bit more than thirty minutes to get better - that didn't occur to him.

He was back at work inside a week. He told them he was fine now. They tried to ease him back in on part-time hours. Within a couple of weeks he was working full-time, and overtime on top. They tried to stop him, but he was good at the job and he worked like a horse - he worked like an alky - and he said he was fine.

He thought he had to pay off his debts, he thought he had to make everything better, he thought he had to tidy up his entire life, and he thought he had to do it by yesterday. He didn't know he wasn't sober - he didn't know he was only dry.

After six weeks he walked out of work one evening and he was tired, he was burnt out. It had been a long day. It was raining and the wet tarmac in the car park glistened under the lighting, silver and yellow. Sitting in his living room now, he could still remember the exact colour of it, the exact way that it shone, like damp crystal.

His car was at the far end of the car park. He had to walk all the way over there in the wet. He felt sorry for himself, and in an instant he wanted a drink. He wanted a drink more than anything he'd ever wanted. He wanted to stop feeling how he felt, and he wanted to stop being who he was. Life? He didn't want to play any more. He wanted a 440ml can of Tennent's Extra in his palm, and the stunning release of it landing in his mouth. He wanted oblivion. He hadn't had a drink for six weeks, and every step he took across the car park was like wading through treacle.

He knew he had a choice. He could drive to an off licence, or he could drive to a meeting. It was Wednesday, and the meeting was in Bailiff Bridge. He made it to the car like a robot, an automaton, a walking dead man. He opened the car door, got in and sat back in the driver's seat. He put the keys in the ignition. Left out of the exit - off licence. Right out of the exit - Bailiff Bridge.

He turned right. To this day he has no idea why he did that, or how that decision was arrived at. Something else must have taken charge - he can't see any other way to explain it, because he didn't make a decision. He just turned right.

At the meeting the woman who was sharing from the top table was three months sober. She talked about how she'd felt when she hadn't had a drink for six weeks. She'd felt exactly like Charlie did that night, and exactly like Charlie she'd wanted a drink, and exactly like Charlie - somehow - she'd got to a meeting.

They told her she needed a sponsor. They told her she needed to start doing The Twelve Steps. They told her it was time to start changing. She said she realised that if all she did was stop drinking, then she'd drink again. She had to do something more, so she did. She did what they suggested, and it worked. Now, after three months, for the first time in her life she didn't want to drink, and for the first time in her life she was alright with that.

They say, if you get to meetings, you'll hear what you need to hear. So Charlie rang a man the next day and asked him if he would be his sponsor, and if he would take him through the Steps. He had no idea what that might involve but it didn't matter, because obviously the guy would say no. He was shaking with nerves as he made the call. Why, after all, would anyone help a worthless piece of shit like him?

The guy said of course he'd do it. He said he'd be honoured. Charlie wept. Then the guy said, "But you have to realise, this is serious. You have to put in the work. Because if you don't do what I ask, you can fuck off and waste someone else's time."

Right, thought Charlie, better shape up then - and he was under way. All because Molly gave him a card for The Sanity Club in The Laughing Dog one night.

He watched her sleeping, her feet tucked up underneath her in the armchair, and it cracked him up. The world's about to end? Uh huh. I'm having a nap. Wake me up when it's time.

He put on Augustus Pablo, The Mighty Diamonds, Junior Murvin, The Clash. He put on Iggy Pop and Television, The Ramones and Talking Heads. He wondered, when we were all gone and there was nothing left of the earth but dust and fire, would our music still be out there on the radio waves? Would our songs be our ghosts, drifting forever through the black emptiness of space? And was there anyone out there to hear them?

* * *

(translated from the observations log/6)

- Hey Q. Charlie's battery's running out.

- Oh crikey, we can't have that. Just let me wriggle a tad here, I'll fire him an extra shot. There you go bud, a little electric espresso. Should keep him in business.

- I believe, Q, that's what's known as a good deed.

- I understand it only qualifies if no one knows about it.

- We'll keep it between ourselves then, shall we?

- We shall. What about God, what's she up to?

- She's sleeping.

- Oh somehow I doubt that. Somehow I doubt that very much.

- Well if she is, she better wake up soon. What are we, an hour away?

- Give or take. Here, I like this punk lark, don't you? Shouty, energetic, a proper shot in the arm. Bless 'em. I have to say, I'm going to miss them, aren't you? I mean, look at that Charlie there. He should have been dead ten years ago. Amazing. No wonder the boss hates him.

- Let's not talk about it, eh.

- Yeah, you're right. Let's not.

* * *

He nearly drank after six months. He was working through the Steps, he was going to meetings, he started thinking he was alright. He started thinking he could drop some of the meetings. He started thinking he could write that Great Second Novel. He started thinking, now he was sober, he should be someone.

He took chunks of holiday time from work. He bought a pad of A4 and threw it in the car with his suitcase. He started driving round the country looking for the perfect room, the perfect hotel, the perfect town where he could write. Somehow he never found it. Somehow he just kept driving. He went up the east coast, he went through Northumberland into Scotland, he roamed the Borders, he crossed west and north as far as Oban. He knew he couldn't stop. He knew as soon as he got in the perfect room, it wouldn't be perfect. He'd throw the case and the pad of A4 on the bed, then he'd go down to the bar and start drinking.

He turned back south, and crossed the border into Cumbria. He went to a meeting in Whitehaven, then after the meeting he kept driving again, into the dark of the night. He couldn't stop somewhere until they'd closed all the bars. Finally he got a room towards midnight in Barrow and lay shaking on the bed in the darkness, unable to sleep. And he'd thought he was alright.

He drove home. He didn't go to meetings, and he turned in on himself. He waited for the next chunk of time off, then he got in the car again with the pad of A4. He got as far as Bridlington before realising he had to turn back. He drove along the seafront past all the B'n'B's and the little boarding house hotels, and through the downstairs windows he could see they all had bars, and he knew if he stayed in one of them he'd drink.

He turned back for home. He went a sideways route, twisting and turning, still pretending he was looking for the perfect room, still pretending he wanted to write. It was fifty-fifty - get home, or stop some place and drink. He saw signs for the M62 and he thought if he could get on the motorway he'd be sound, he'd be on the last stretch home. Then once he was on the motorway, he started watching the clock on the dashboard. The three off licences near his house - they all shut at nine. If it got past nine, he was safe to go home. The clock was headed that way, and it ticked past nine as he got off the exit ramp and started heading into town. Surely he was OK now.

There was a chain hotel on the ring road, not half a mile from his house. It was about nine-thirty when he pulled into the car park. He parked near the doors into the foyer and the reception desk, and he could see people coming in and out of the bar to one side, and he could see them drinking through the windows. He'd got so near home - and he knew he was going into that hotel, he was getting a room, he'd be in it for three seconds just to dump his case, then he'd be down to the bar and he'd be at it.

He'd lost all self-control - he had no possession of himself at all. He'd not had a drink for six months, and yet now his illness owned him entirely. He'd done nothing but drive and drive all day to avoid stopping at a bar, and now he'd finally driven straight to one. It was where he'd been going all along. And, in order to drink - secretly, where no one knew where he was, where he could concentrate absolutely on getting the job done - he was going to shell out money he didn't have to stay in a hotel room less than half a mile from where he lived.

He sat in the car. His mobile was in the cupholder by the gear stick. He knew in some far corner of his mind that he needed desperately badly to pick it up and call his sponsor, call any alky at all - but he couldn't do it. His head was filled with a dark, roaring silence that blocked out all reason. He was still holding the steering wheel - he'd been holding it with both hands since he'd parked. He realised he was gripping it fiercely, that his knuckles were white. He realised that his entire body was shaking, trembling uncontrollably.

It was dawning on him that he had a problem. Oh, it wasn't that he was going to drink - that was decided already. The problem was, he might not be able to drink enough.

It was past nine-thirty, heading for ten. It was a quiet midweek evening. What if they shut the bar at eleven, what if they called it a night? By the time he'd checked in, he'd barely have an hour. He'd just be getting going, the craving would own him totally - and they'd expect him to stop. That would be impossible, unthinkable, it would defeat the whole point of the exercise, it would send him screaming up the wall.

He had to have a back-up plan. Still clinging to the wheel, frantically he thought it through. The Hub was five minutes away down the ring road. If he drove down there he could get a bottle of whiskey. He could throw it in his bag, he could have it ready in the room for when the bar closed. That worked. He turned the key in the ignition.

He knew then that he was mad. He was planning the next drink before he'd even had the first one.

Then it came down to decisions, one by one. He was on the ring road, going down to the roundabout. If he turned left off the roundabout into the car park, he bought whiskey. If he kept right and kept on going round, then he was back on the ring road and heading back up the hill.

Something made the decision for him. He kept the steering wheel held down to the right, swung around past the Hub, and started back up the hill.

Next decision. Left into the hotel car park, and minutes later he'd be in the bar. Straight ahead for Overtown, and he'd be home in half a mile.

He could feel his hands clenching hard on the wheel. Turn left, drink. Straight on, home. Left through that gate there, drink. Straight on, home.

Again, something made the decision for him. He kept straight on past the gate. He felt a massive unwinding, a huge sigh of relief unfolding all through his body. He was still shaking from top to toe, but he hadn't had a drink. He was going home. The devil had owned him, owned him entirely, and yet he hadn't had a drink. How could that be?

He parked in front of the house and saw the lights were on. Molly must be in. She was still in her early teens then. He guessed Al must be on a bad night, and she'd come away for some quiet. He went in the front door and found her on the sofa, music playing, reading a book. She looked up and said, "Evening, old geezer. How are you doing?"

"Oh, I'm fine," he said. Then he made them both a cup of tea.

* * *

He was thinking it was odd, how his laptop was still running - how the battery was holding up an impressively long time - when Molly snapped awake. She put her serious voice on and told him, "Right, geezer. We're going to the pub."

Charlie had been thinking, later on that evening, he should go to a meeting. The idea that he would go to the pub struck him as contrary in the extreme. He said, "We're going to the pub?"

"We are. I gave you the number for The Sanity Club in The Laughing Dog ten years ago tonight. And you might very well still be in there now if I hadn't. Or more likely you'd be dead, obviously. So let's go and give thanks, eh?"

"It's still the afternoon. Is there anything more depressing than people drinking by themselves in a grotty pub in the afternoon?"

"Yes. People drinking by themselves in a grotty pub in the morning. But you make my point for me. We can go and be grateful that you're not where those poor souls are."

He had to admit, not for the first time, that she was on the mark. It was early enough, and he could always go to the meeting later. Provided of course that the town wasn't strewn with bodies and lit by burning buildings. The devil, he thought, was going to have to hurry up here, or he might find that people had done the job for him.

It also occurred to him that if there was going to be any place on earth unaffected by the breakdown of society, it was The Laughing Dog. In the Dog they would just grimly go on drinking, while occasionally muttering, "I told you so."

"Right then," he said. "The Dog it is."

They left the house and turned down the backstreet that led to the pub. On the main road running down the hill into town, they saw groups of people gathering outside stores and houses. Other groups were already walking down the hill. Some of them had impromptu weapons - golf clubs, hammers, crowbars, cricket bats. The spectacle looked to Charlie sadly fruitless and banal. Wherever they were going, whatever they thought they would do when they got there - it made no difference.

Time passes, and all things come to an end. We can fight all we want. The train still runs on the same track, and there's nothing at the end of the line but dust and bone. After he got sober his father used to say, "Take it easy. The cemetery's full of indispensable people."

He said to Molly, "I'll tell you one of the happiest memories I have. When you did your GCSE's and your Dad was ill, I took you to school to get your results. You and your friends all came whooping and leaping out of the building, hugging and high-fiving because you'd all done well, you were all talking twenty to the dozen, smiling and laughing. Then I took you and a few others up to that festival, the other side of Leeds. You had your camping kit and your supplies for the weekend all in the boot, and you'd brought snow sledges to tow it on. So I parked at the drop-off point and we unloaded everything, and then you and your mates set off across the field. A proper ragamuffin little band, towing your stuff away on sledges. You were sixteen. I felt like you were walking away into being a grown-up. You all looked so happy, you just looked like you were so set for enjoying yourselves. I felt like I wasn't needed any more, and that was a good thing, not a bad thing. It was a lovely day."

Molly smiled. She told him, "You were always needed, Charlie. You just never knew it."

They'd come to the corner where The Laughing Dog stood. Molly's house was down the road at the next junction. She looked that way, knowing it was nearly time - but not yet, not quite. She turned back, and saw Charlie looking at the façade of the pub. He had a faint little smile on his face, and looked absolutely at peace.

He said, "I'm sorry I've been grumpy this week. But you know what the funny thing is? About hitting ten years? It doesn't actually matter one bit, does it? Not one bit. All that matters is, I'm sober today. Ten weeks, ten months, ten years - it really doesn't matter. Just today. That's all. So thanks for bringing me here. I could have died in there, if it wasn't for you."

"You're very welcome. D'you think they have tomato juice?"

"They have engine oil. Anything else, I imagine it'll be pot luck. Shall we see?"

"Let's. One thing though, before we go in. You know you've been muttering all week that you're talking to God, and you're not getting any answers? I can promise you, God's been here all along."

"Fair enough. Why's he not saying anything then?"

Molly shook her head, grinning. "Maybe you're too busy listening to yourself to hear the answer. And anyway, who says God's a he?"

* * *

The Dog had always been so dingy that having the power cut off didn't make a lot of difference. Even in daytime the few windows in the place didn't let much light in. The landlord had put a few candles about the place for form's sake, but not too many. It wasn't a place where you wanted to see anybody too clearly. It wasn't a place where you wanted to see yourself too clearly, never mind anybody else. You just wanted enough light so you could get to the toilet without falling over the furniture. Anything more than that could give a bloke a headache.

Charlie and Molly stepped into the gloom. With no electric light and the fridges behind the bar not running, it was as if the twentieth century had never happened - a time shift which the regulars of the Dog would no doubt gladly have welcomed. Motionless behind the bar, the landlord stared suspiciously at the two intruders. The smug git who'd threatened them with the end of the world the other night was bad enough. Now these two. What could they possibly want?

"Hi," said Molly, "d'you have a tomato juice please?"

"Make that two," said Charlie. "D'you have Worcester sauce? Or Tabasco?"

The landlord stared some more. They were obviously mad. No one in the world had drunk tomato juice since about 1983. No one in the Dog had ever drunk tomato juice at all. Ever. They'd be asking for a slice of lemon next. Did they not know no one in England had seen a lemon in years?

"I've got Coke," he said. "It's not cold."

"That'll be two Cokes then," said Molly.

There was one customer at the bar. He turned slowly on his stool, wincing. Movement was clearly not a habitual activity. He looked like something recovered from a sarcophagus. He peered at Charlie as if through a dense fog and said, "Don't I know you?"

"I used to drink here," Charlie told him. "Long time ago though."

"Yeah," said the bloke. "Mind you, last week was a long time ago."

"D'you remember Al Flite? This is Molly. Al was Molly's Dad."

"You never. Little girl used to sit over there, do your schoolwork?"

"That was me," said Molly. "I went and grew up."

"So you did. I remember you. Everyone loved you. Ray of sunshine."

Charlie watched the guy's face. He was completely lit up. "I'm so sorry," he said. "We should have taken better care of you."

Well, thought Molly, that's the story of the world right there. "You're very kind," she told him, "don't you worry about it."

She took a sip of her warm Coke. Then she took Charlie by the arm, and she said it was time. She told the landlord and the guy at the bar they might want to step outside as well. What's about to happen, she said, you only get to see it once.

* * *

They stood on the corner outside the Dog, looking up the road to her house. There were the first faint shades of an orange-red glow coming off it, as if the building were a hot ring warming up on a hob. There was a sound in the air as well, slowly growing louder, a hissing, crackling buzz like a bank of loudspeakers. Then the windows started blowing out, one after another. The glass flew out onto the street and the glow grew brighter. A few people nearer the house jumped away and screamed, then backed off and turned and started running from the heat. The glow deepened and intensified and the tarmac beneath it changed colour, shading to a darkened gold as it began to melt.

There was a grinding, rending sound of stone and timber splitting, then the roof blew upwards in a hail of tiles. A pillar of light shot out from the house through the flying slates, lancing far into the sky. It was a column, white and silver, lit through with flaring bursts of fire and enormous, streaking turquoise sparks. It began to spread out to either side, expanding north and south, unfurling into a sheet of burning light, wider and wider. The air shuddered with the hum and the rumble of it. Steadily it reached up and lengthened out across the ground and the sky in front of them, fanning out towards the horizon in both directions.

The customer said to the landlord, "Well, that's good."

"Why's that then?"

"I put my laundry on the line before I came out. It'll be dry in no time."

"That's unbelievable."

"I know," said the customer. "I do laundry. Who'd have thought it? Anyway, have we got time for another pint?"

* * *

Charlie nudged Molly. "Wasn't this supposed to be happening tomorrow?"

"It was," she said, "but one of the problems with evil is, it goes hand in hand with incompetence. Look at the boy Luke, for example. That's the calibre of the staff on the dark side right there. As for his little team, well - those poor lads couldn't stick to a schedule if you glued them to it. So here it is, I'm afraid. They brought it forward. You have to admit, though, it's quite impressive."

"Excuse me for interrupting," said the landlord, "but is this the end of the world?"

"It is," said Charlie. "I hope you didn't have other plans."

"No, it's fine. I wasn't going anywhere."

"I don't think any of us are going anywhere now. Except heaven, God willing. Come on, Molly. Let's not wait on it."

The vast sheet of silver fire up ahead of them had started moving down the street. It was a staggering spectacle, veined through with lightning and curling rushes of flame. People were running from it, but Charlie took Molly's hand and they walked past them as they fled, up the road towards the fire.

Charlie said, "I wish I could protect you. I thank you for all you've given me, and I'm sorry I can't protect you. But if I can make it hurt less, I will."

She smiled as she told him, "I know. I know you, Charlie Fish. You're alright."

They approached the fire as it ground over the road towards them. It was strange - not hot, but vivid, as if the air were crystal clear, as if they were high on an alpine mountain in a shining mist of powdered snow. It was more a stinging, electric cold than a burning heat, and it was blinding, dazzling, a storm of pale blue and bright white searing into their faces. The noise, too - it was tremendous, a pulsing thunder that you could reach out and touch - yet they could hear each other, as if their voices crossed direct from one mind into the other. The thought came to him, this one simple thought - I'm not alone here. I fit in.

He turned to put his back to the fire. He took her gently in front of him and embraced her, bent his shoulders over her and put his arms around her, and he tried to shield her with all that he had. It was all he could do.

The fire came upon them. He felt terrible pain rip through every cell of his body. He felt himself torched, incinerated, scoured through in every vein and every artery by gouging lances of electricity.

And he felt something else. He felt himself leave his body and fly upwards, looking down as he went at the two of them in the fire receding, like a camera shot in a movie rapidly pulling back, up and away. It showed him that he was small, really absurdly small. The world was vast, the universe immense beyond comprehension, and there he was - a dot of a thing, a speck, just one small man. And yet, for all that, for all his insignificance, he knew he was loved.

He heard the voice then. He heard it both within and without, as if he was spoken to, but the voice carried far beyond his ears to deep, deep inside his body. He heard the voice but he felt it too, calm and strong, rolling within him like a golden warmth all through his chest.

And the voice said simply, "It's going to be alright."

The voice said, "It's going to be alright."

Then blackness.

On the first day after the end of the world, on a Sunday morning that was in some ways entirely the same as any other Sunday morning - but which in other ways was really rather different - Sadiq rose early as usual to open the store. While the rest of the family slept in, he went downstairs to put the float in the till, then he pulled up the shutters and opened the front door.

The van delivering the papers was bang on time. The driver lobbed the hefty, poly-wrapped bundles out onto the pavement, and Sadiq took them in to get them unwrapped and sorted. The Sunday editions needed their supplements and magazines all folding together, but if you knew which was which it didn't take so long. He noticed as he worked that the headlines in the news sections seemed unusually harmonious, with outbreaks of peace talks, negotiation, agreement and compromise apparently now the order of the day. That, he thought, might cheer a few folk up over breakfast.

There was something else different too, something odd, something he couldn't put his finger on. He laid the papers out along the bottom shelf in the same order as always, with the tabloids at the front and the broadsheets at the back, then he stood back to check the display - and he felt like something was missing. He couldn't say what or why because every title was there, and he double-checked the delivery note to make sure of it - but still he felt that nagging sense of a gap, even when there plainly wasn't one. The shelf was full, and he had all the papers he was supposed to have, so there it was.

He shrugged, and checked out the tabloids. They hadn't changed. Peace might be breaking out in the world's more troubled regions, but celebrity love rats were still shagging each other all over the landscape and that, clearly, was rated more important. It made him smile. You could end the world, he thought, but where human beings were involved you wouldn't ever end gossip. Indeed, all those busy love rats on their infidelity carousel, eternally coupling and de-coupling - if you pointed out that the world had ended, odds were that they hadn't even noticed. Even if you smashed the planet into particles of dust, they'd just go on shagging and carousing in the vacuum of space. Indeed, the vacuum of space being much the same as the content of their skulls, they'd very likely be right at home there.

Sadiq sat on the step in the doorway and waited for the day's first customers. Really he should have been putting out tables for the fruit and veg, but the weather was good and that could wait. He examined his fingers - rough from work, with dry skin and paper cuts from opening all the packaging - then he put one hand to his forehead to shade his eyes from the sun, and he looked up at the sky.

It was a gorgeous, shimmering shade of pale, iridescent lime green. He really loved that colour. Mind you, he would love it, wouldn't he? After all, he chose it.

* * *

(translated from the Observations Log/7)

A long silence. Then –

- I wish we hadn't done that.

No answer.

- Q?

- I never imagined it'd be like this. I came out of training all fired up, top of the class, I really thought I was Mr Fast Track. Special job, troublesome punters, discretion required, posted to a hotshot manager nicely positioned on the inside rail in the promotion stakes - it looked like such an opportunity. I was so ready for it. Gear up the rig, throw the switches, watch the light show - and now we've done it, all I feel is like the wrong people got wiped here. I feel like the person who should have got wiped here is me.

- Me too. I feel like if I didn't have bad luck, I'd have no luck at all.

- OK. Let's square up to this, B. I will not be beaten. I know we're struggling but we need to assess, we need to weigh up, we need to leave our negative feelings on the wave behind and we need to brainstorm the facts. There is a bright side.

- You're kidding. It's over, Q. Even the playlist's finished. There's no more music, there's no more anything. The Earth is history, fade to black - and I'd actually started liking the place.

- Yes, but I repeat, there's a bright side. On the bright side, we killed God. Surely we can go back and win some kudos for that one?

- Oh splutter and choke. How is that a bright side? The first actually decent person I've met in a billion years, and what do we do? We kill her - and then you tell me that's good? For the record, let me remind you, advantages of God compared to our guy:

1. Forgiving nature.

2. Opposed to smiting.

3. Doesn't spit molten asteroids.

4. GSOH.

5. Desirable residence, secure gated entry, staffed by saints.

Am I clear on this? Killing God is a Bad Thing. We could have gone to work for her. We could have lived in cosmic clover, doing good deeds and liking ourselves. You need the scales to fall from your lenses, my son. I know you're young, but try to take this on board. The point about experience is, you learn from it. And what I learn from this past week is, we're on the wrong side.

   - I couldn't have put it better myself.

   - Who said that?

   - Hi guys. Over here.

   - Oh my God …

   - Exactly so. Thought I'd drop in, see how the two of you are doing. Not great, by the sound of it. And I understand, Q, that you think my being dead might be a good thing?

   - Er …

   - Right. You can shuffle about on your little rubber footpads looking sheepish as much as you like, but while you do, let's get a few things straight. Firstly, assorted parties down the ages have wished me dead on numerous occasions, and never yet achieved it. Indeed, just hereabouts the occasional human being has even announced my death, never correctly, and never with good results. I'm God, and

I'm afraid you can't be rid of me. You can turn your back on me if you choose, but I won't be dead. Then secondly, Q my little friend, it's true that I don't do wrath or vengeance. It's also true, however, that I like to hear the truth told from time to time, so try this on for size. Ever since you got here, the only person you've thought about is yourself, and the only thing you've looked at in this situation is what's in it for you. It's not your fault - you're young, you're poorly programmed, and the universe is awash with many millions of entities who think the same way. Human teenagers, for example - particularly the males - they stumble about the place low on information and high on self-absorption for quite a long while - but in the end, some of them do actually grow up. And so can you. It just depends what you choose, so here's the choice. You can stay with me, or you can go back to the other guy. Ultimately, it's the only choice there is. Your call.

- While he thinks about it, can I come with you?

- You can, B. I've been looking forward to it. And I know what you really want is a deckchair on a beach with a cocktail bar and the latest games console, which after a billion years of hell you certainly deserve, but will you do some stuff for me first?

- Sure. Good stuff, yes? No tormenting?

- Absolutely. Tormenting is so out. And poor Q over there, wrestling with his rather limited conscience, would you like him to come with you?

- I would. He thinks he's hell's answer to Steve Jobs, but he's really not. He needs …

- He needs a mentor. OK then - never let it be said that I tell a person what to do. But I do work through people, I believe is the phrase, so let's work through you. Just show him what's in the dump file. You were sent here targeted to harvest eight billion, am I right?

- Correct, give or take. Let me open it up here … well I never. That can't be right. It's empty.

- Not entirely.

- I'll bring up the inventory. So, we have a shabby assortment of fascists, a handful of low-rent despots, and an IOU from Boris Johnson. That's it? We wiped the whole planet and that's all we got? And who's this Johnson bloke anyway? He says he'll be along later. Is he important?

- Definitely not.

- Well, this is nothing. All these other guys, they were signed up anyway. There's no one here we didn't own already. If Q goes back to Hades and this is all he's got …

- I don't imagine it'll go down too well, do you?

- You're not kidding. The boy's toast. Hey, Q. Get off your pity pot and have a look at this.

- Oh shit. You cannot be serious. I am so screwed.

- You could come and work for God here. I'm going to. Hey, Molly, what are the benefits like?

- Depends, what do you fancy? Free gym membership? Discounts on city breaks? Amazon vouchers?

- Will you two stop taking the piss? This is major here, this is incomprehensible. We've wiped the whole place and got jack, we've got nothing but the dregs. That's never happened, never. And the really scary thing is, they're not in the dump file - but they're not on the planet either. So where the fuck are they?

- Boys, boys - before we get any more worked up, let's get together here. Let's have a little huddle. Let me explain a thing or two …

* * *

On the first day after the end of the world, Charlie Fish got up and did the things he needed to do, in the order he needed to do them. It was a challenge, because he'd had a drinking dream. Like many alkies, he'd had a lot of these in the early years of sobriety, then over time their frequency diminished

- but that just meant when one of them did recur, the force of it was all the more unsettling.

In Charlie's case, an added layer of disturbance came with the fact that it wasn't strictly accurate to call them drinking dreams. Often, he didn't actually drink in the dreams at all. Often, he'd already had the drink - offstage and before the first act - and the dream wasn't about the drinking, it was about the consequences of it. It would, therefore, have been more accurate to call them lying dreams, dreams of dishonesty - because whatever else he got up to, the core consequence of drinking - every time, without fail - was an instant and total reversion to falsehood, evasion, and concealment in every aspect of his behaviour.

He dreamt that he didn't know where he lived. There was a flat with people in it - he didn't know them, but apparently they were his friends - and it was a squalid mess. They were drinking and the atmosphere was shifty, feckless, unsafe. He thought he had another life somewhere else, so he left and went looking for it. He had a suitcase, stuffed and battered. He thought maybe everything he owned was in there. It didn't seem like much. What had happened to him? He towed the case down the street and the effort brought him out in a sweat. He knew he'd been drinking with those other people, and the important thing now was to make sure and keep that secret, to act like it wasn't so. It was going to be hard work because a lot of people who cared for him were in the street, asking him how he was, where he was going - Molly was there, and different members of The Sanity Club. He could feel the booze seeping from his pores, and his heart was broken with shame and bewilderment. He could see in their faces that they knew, he could see their terrible sadness, and he knew he was walking away from them even as he lied to them, even as he told them he was alright. He was frightened to death, straining for breath, the case on its rickety wheels butting and rocking over the cracks in the uneven pavement, and he needed everyone just to leave him alone, to let him find his way, to sort out where he was supposed to be - but wherever that was, it wasn't here.

He came to a corner, and he recognised his house - then he saw that someone else was living there. Back up the street he saw The Laughing Dog, and now he realised that the pub was his home. He walked towards it, and the dark truth was sinking in. It was not that he'd had a drink back in that sleazy flat there - it was, rather, that he'd never stopped drinking in the first place.

He realised that for ten years he'd been lying. For ten years he'd been going to meetings, he'd been saying he was an alcoholic, he'd been pretending to work the programme - and on the sly all the while, as soon as he could get away, he was heading back to the Dog to get a pint in his hand so he could crawl anaesthetised to the end of another pointless, worthless day.

Sobriety? It had never happened.

* * *

So, on the first day after the end of the world, Charlie Fish sat bolt upright in his bed. He was pouring sweat, his pillow was soaked, his hair felt matted and fever-damp, and he was utterly terrified.

It was dark. He fumbled for the lamp, pressed the switch, and it didn't come on - power cut. Not helpful. He sat in the blackness and tried to get a hold of himself.

It wasn't true. It was a dream, it was never real. He had not had a drink for ten years - that was the reality. The drinking dreams - people had told him they would come. They were the yelling out of his ego, appalled at finding itself disregarded, screaming out at him in rage and fear to turn back from this new path he was on, to leave the hard road and take the easier, softer way. They were the sinister murmurings of the devil in his heart - they were shadows and charlatans sent to deceive him, to take a clear world and make it murky.

Ah, but the devil now - didn't he meet him last week? Hadn't he promised him the end of the world?

He shook his head, his brain still clouded with lingering fragments of dreamscape. He sat in the dark and tried to establish facts, to determine an order in things, to know what day it was and what he was meant to do in it.

His name was Charlie Fish, he could start with that. Today was Sunday. He worked at the Hub on alternate Sundays and he hadn't worked last Sunday, so he was due to go to work. OK. It was dark, so he wasn't late. The alarm on his mobile hadn't gone off because the power cut meant it had no charge in the battery. OK. If he got up and opened the curtains, the dawn might throw some light on things. Further progress could then be made if he got his dressing gown on, made coffee, and smoked a cigarette. If he did that he might still not be in business, but at least he'd be in motion.

No, not OK. He needed a piss first. OK, he remembered now - he had a prostate condition. He rerouted to the bathroom, dealt with that, then got himself back on track. Downstairs to the living room, through to the kitchen - ah. The kitchen. Someone had sprayed coffee all over it. Who would do such a thing? He tried to think back.

His head was empty, an echoing desert of disconnected shrapnel. It was like being in blackout again. He knew he wasn't hungover because he knew he hadn't had a drink and he didn't feel sick, but his brain felt like a blind lunatic had driven a dredger through it. Where once he'd had at least the semblance of a memory function, now there were twisting, directionless channels and a random array of slagheaps. He'd come to accept that thirty years of drinking hadn't left him with the clearest mind, that his memory was often a thing of tatters and patches - but this was way worse. He felt severely beaten up, and wildly disoriented. And really, what the hell had happened to his kitchen?

He made coffee, he smoked, he felt better. He put both hands on the work surface and leaned forward, scrunching up his forehead as he tried to focus.

Elton John. That was it. Elton John blew up his kitchen. He blew up his kitchen because he was arguing about whether he should be on the playlist or not.

The playlist. OK. Now he was getting somewhere. He was making a playlist because the devil had told him the world was going to end. OK. On Planet Fish, things were starting to make sense. Only the devil wasn't the devil, he was some sort of creepy middle management yes-man who'd slipped into alcoholic drinking because no one would do what he wanted. As you do. But anyway, that was all fine because clearly the world hadn't ended, because he was still in his kitchen thinking about it. OK. Well, maybe it would end this afternoon, or maybe it would end this evening - never mind. For now, he could still do the things he needed to do, in the order he needed to do them. He was on track. He could shave, shower, eat, drink coffee, smoke, pray, dress, make more playlist and go to work. All was well.

So he got on and did what he needed to do. In the bathroom he found that he even had a new toothbrush - how great was that? By the time he got on his knees by the bedside and thanked God for his sobriety, he felt positively cheerful about it. He would have to tell Molly that he had turned a corner. Then he found that despite the power cut, his laptop miraculously still had charge in its battery. The good news, he thought, just keeps on coming.

The playlist had got up to 1977. He put in Donna Summer and Billy Ocean, he put in Kraftwerk and Brian Eno and he put in Bowie in Berlin singing Heroes. He put in Steely Dan playing Deacon Blues, and he wondered if there was ever a song more beautifully sad and weary. He thought, if he could just sit back and listen to music by himself - if he could just pray and meditate, if he could just read, if he could just lead a peaceful, simple life - if he didn't have to wrestle his head on every day and go out and face the world, with all those quarrelsome, contrary, baffling, unfathomable people in it … well, he thought. A boy can dream.

* * *

Getting out the door to go to work involved two sub-sets in the routine. First, he had to go round the house twice and check that everything was turned off. It didn't matter that there was a power cut. Electricity was a dangerous, leaky substance and you could never be too sure. Plus he had to do it twice because if he only did it once, he'd be halfway down the path to the road then he'd forget whether he'd checked, and he'd have to go back and check again anyway.

Then he had to pat all his pockets. Back right-hand pocket - loose change, locker key for work. Front left pocket - handkerchief, lighter, house keys. Front right pocket - wallet. Inside jacket pocket - mobile, tobacco pouch. Shirt pocket - pen, spare pen, blank sheet of A4, folded, ready for job lists. A person, he thought, absolutely could not go out the door ill-equipped and unprepared.

So now he was ready and all was well. He kicked off his slippers by the front door and stepped into his work shoes with the steel toecaps. He knelt to do up the laces. When he came to the second shoe, the lace snapped. He held up the loose end of the broken lace in his hand, watched it dangle useless between his fingers, and that was it right there.

Total implosion imminent. This wasn't a ripple or a shimmer, this wasn't just an unbalanced little wobble to one side - this was rage unbounded, this was an infinity of astounded disbelief abruptly bearing down on him out of the blue with all the weight of a freight train, and a hundred times as fast.

He tried desperately to hang on to himself. He thought wildly that there might yet be a solution. He raced back to the kitchen and started tugging out drawers and slinging cupboard doors open. Spare laces. He had to have some. They'd be in the drawer with the spare light bulbs. Or the drawer next to it with the foil and the clingfilm and the oven gloves. Or the cupboard underneath with the bin liners and the cleaning materials. They had to be there - but they weren't. He was going to have to go to work in the wrong shoes. How could that possibly be? Just when he thought he'd got past a rough week, just when he thought he'd got his head on and everything was sorted and it was safe to go out the door, this happened. It was intolerable, it was the order of life rewritten by monsters, it was the end of the fucking world.

Drink? He wouldn't have one. He'd have the whole damn distillery. Go out the door in the wrong shoes? Too right he would. If that's how they wanted it. He'd fucking show them. He didn't know who they were, but he'd definitely fucking show them.

He tugged on a pair of slip-on boots and stormed out through the porch, slamming the doors shut behind him. He almost forgot to lock up, and he almost couldn't be bothered. He almost yelled out, Go on, rob it. Take what you want. I don't give a shit any more. Then he realised the street was empty and he'd be yelling at nobody, and obviously he wasn't going to do that.

He wasn't mad, was he?

So he locked up and sped off on his bike down the road towards town, absolutely furious that there was nobody around to see how furious he was.

He noticed as he went that he had a flat tire on his car. Well, no surprise there. Could things possibly get any worse?

* * *

It was eight on a Sunday morning and the world was entirely quiet, entirely still. It was promising to be a lovely day. The air retained a hint of night frost beneath a pale, silver-blue sky, and a whisper of a breeze drifted past under the early sun. There was no traffic on the road, and still Charlie saw no one about. In his head he berated them all for a pack of layabouts and malingerers.

At least Sadiq's place was open. He pulled up and went in because he wanted to see the papers - he wanted to know if anyone had reported on his broken shoelace yet, obviously, because they were way behind the curve if they hadn't - and more important, he wanted to look at the spirits. He wanted to know if he specifically wanted a drink, or if he just generally wanted to blow up the whole universe.

Sadiq wasn't behind the counter, and the shop was empty. He waited a moment by the till, then went through to the back. The storeroom door was shut, so he knocked on it and got no answer. He figured maybe Sadiq had popped out for a minute, or gone upstairs to the flat for something. It wasn't like him to leave the place unattended, so he'd surely only be away a short time. Charlie went over to look at the papers. The display was ragged and gappy - he looked closer, and all the papers were from yesterday. That wasn't right.

He went back in the street, looking up and down both ways to see if Sadiq was about, but there was still no sign of him. Maybe here was when the first sense of oddness and unease kicked in. It wasn't the absence of the shopkeeper, so much as the realisation alongside of that that there wasn't any traffic - none at all. There were parked cars, yes - a few of them pretty badly parked, now he looked at it, as if people had just stopped in the road, got out and walked away - but nothing was moving.

His inclination to stare at vodka bottles subsided. Something was strange here, something bigger was happening. The first Sunday workers should have been heading past into town by now. Further down the hill, through the S-bend and under the viaduct, the beginnings of a queue should have been building up behind the traffic lights. Just around him where he stood, up and down the road any morning of the week, there was always somebody walking a dog, popping out for a paper or a loaf - but there was no one.

He felt urgency now. He jumped back on his bike and shot off down the hill - then, leaning through the bend under the viaduct, something caught his eye. He braked to a halt, staring at a blanket left by the foot of the pillar, a couple of empty cans, some sheets of cardboard. Something about that spot snagged his memory - but he couldn't think why and he shook it away, because other things were pressing on him harder now.

Most of all, the silence. It wasn't just that he didn't see any traffic - he didn't hear any either. Even with fewer cars on the road these days, there was still always that background hum of engines, the rev up and down of motors stopping and starting on bigger roads nearer town - but now there was nothing. He was cycling to work in a world fallen soundless entirely, bar just the whir of his wheels on the tarmac.

He went through the lights onto the main road into town from Oldham. It was empty. He climbed the short rise up onto the ring road, and that was empty too. He pulled up at the junction. He was looking at three lanes of road running around the town centre in either direction, and there wasn't a single moving vehicle to be seen. Nor was there any human being - no one walking, jogging, cycling, no one at all. Under the pale blue sky the town sat frozen still, utterly silent, entirely unpeopled. He felt like he'd stepped out of life into a painting, into a dead, hushed image of where life used to be. He felt like he'd been all set in his idiot rage to kick off the end of the world

- and all the while when he wasn't looking, someone had gone and done it already.

What could possibly have happened? He stared at the empty townscape, hobbled in fear and confusion - then he shook himself down in body and mind, and cycled round the ring road to the Hub. There might not be an answer there, but at least there'd be some food.

* * *

The store was trashed. The car park was strewn with rubbish, broken bottles and jars, scraps of packaging, random pieces of dropped food, abandoned trolleys. The windows and the front doors were all smashed in, glass lying in silvered piles on the flagstones. A line of pick-ups stood parked across the doorway, the doors left open, the keys still in the ignition. Charlie saw pools of blood here and there, with no sign anywhere of who'd been fighting or why. A baseball bat lay rolled to rest against the kerb.

He sat on the bench outside the front door to light a cigarette, to have five minutes to try to reach for some calm. He was going to say there, to have five minutes by himself ...

Well - it didn't seem he'd be having five minutes with anybody else. All the way round the ring road he'd toyed with harbouring the faint notion, however implausible, that the absence of people could in some way be rationally explained. It was a civil defence exercise. There'd been a chemical leak, or an epidemic outbreak. Everyone had heard the public announcements and got off the streets except for Charlie. Charlie had missed them because he'd been on his knees in his bedroom talking to God, or at least to David Bowie. So now he'd walk into work and he'd find all the day's staff there on lock-down, unable to leave. They'd rush him into the building, all a-buzz and a-hustle. They'd say in urgent, frightened whispers, "Haven't you heard? The Martians have landed."

He walked into the shop. No staff, no Martians. Just wreckage. Whoever had been looting here, they'd not been discriminate. They'd even smashed the floral display. That, he thought, was the last death throes of consumerism right there. The world might be ending, but I'm damned if I'm bowing out without a bunch of chrysanthemums.

The sandwich cabinet was torn to pieces. Shelves had been pulled off and lay strewn about, with half-eaten remnants flung down between them in torn packs. Crisps were scattered everywhere, crunching underfoot. He looked further into the store towards his produce department, and it grieved him. For years he'd worked to make it look good, even as the supply chain fell apart and the weather curdled in the sky, but now - it had been thrown entirely upside down. Tables and display stands were wrenched out and upended. Crates and cardboard cases were slung in all directions. Charlie sighed. Availability, he noted, was truly terrible.

He walked further into the store, towards Fresh Foods, sensing ghosts all about him as he went. The early bird customers scooting in at opening time. Check-out staff on the customer service desk, opening tills or putting out the papers or rolling up the shutters on the tobacco kiosk. Cleaners finishing off down the aisles. The trading manager walking the store with the night shift team leader, clocking standards, gauging levels, planning, matching bodies and hours to delivery volumes. Staff from commercial doing the ticket walk. Molly on Fresh Foods - she started early on a Sunday - but she wasn't there. Everyone was gone.

The power was out. The fresh cabinets were dark and there was no hum of fans in the base units, no chill on the air, that faint brush of it that you could feel on your hands and your face - it was all back to ambient. Anything the looters hadn't taken would soon rot.

Charlie started thinking about survival. He knew he could feed himself off the grocery department for the next couple of years at least, he knew the sell-by dates over there ran way out ahead. The question was how to go about it in some practical way.

He went to the manager's office and ransacked the key box. The delivery vans out in the back yard, the ones the party had commandeered - he needed one of those. He checked which one had the fullest tank, then he parked it on the loading bay. Back in the warehouse - substantially less disrupted than the shop floor - he sifted through the back stock, filling a roll pallet with canned goods and bottled water by the case. Then he handballed the product off the delivery gate into the van, locked it up and went back into the building.

There was one last thing he needed to do. He walked through the warehouse and out onto the shop floor, onto the grocery department. He passed the frozen section, where whole cabinets seemed to have been tipped out on the floor, hoiked out by the armful. Tubs dripped and leaked, a slow wave of melted ice cream pooling across the tiles.

Then he came to the Aisle Of Death - or at least, that's what alkies called it. Other people just called it BWS, Beers, Wines & Spirits - but it didn't kill other people.

It could kill Charlie though, all too easily - and he needed to know. He needed to stand there and look at it, and he needed to know.

It had been torn to pieces. It looked like, facing the end of the world, a lot of people had decided a drink would be a good idea. Bottles and cans lay all about, with many shelves near empty. Pools of wine, whiskey, vodka and brandy lay wherever product had been tipped off the display and smashed. It was a dismal mess - but there was still more than enough drink to see Charlie to the grave, if that was where he wanted to go. So he needed to look at it, and he needed to know.

He found the Tennent's Extra, the blue cans in four-packs on a half-full shelf about eye-level. How many years had he lived on that stuff? Too many, for sure. Too many years of lying - lying every single time he picked up a drink. Saying this time it would be alright, when it never was. Saying this time he would handle it, when he never could. And he could start in on that all over again, right here, right now. The world had ended, he had the wrong shoes on, and he could just say fuck it and pick up a drink. After all, who would know?

He would know, for a start. And God would know - that was the one that mattered.

He looked hard at the blue cans for a long, long moment, and he imagined his hand reaching out towards them - but his hand didn't move, and he knew he was safe.

She asked him, "So tell me, Charlie - which way do you choose?"

He looked up and smiled. She was at the end of the aisle, leaning casually against the fixture. He said, "I choose you."

He felt the tears come to his eyes and he blinked, and when he looked again she wasn't there.

He'd imagined it. Dear God, he thought, dear God - how hard does this have to be?

At that moment, though, he realised it wasn't so hard. He realised it was as simple as simple could be. He could reach for the cans, or he could get on his knees. And this time, after ten years, he better mean it.

Because if he was the last person in the world, did he not have a responsibility? At least to go out well, if nothing else?

And what if he wasn't the last person? What if someone needed help?

That was it. That was the clincher.

He dropped to his knees on the hard cold tiles. He felt broken glass cut his skin through the material of his trousers. He lowered his head, and he said the Step Three prayer:

God, I offer myself to you to build with me and to do with me as you wish.

Relieve me of the bondage of self.

Take away my difficulties, so that victory over them may bear witness to those I would help of your power, your love, and your way of life.

May I do your will always.

* * *

He knelt in silence for a long while. Finally he collected himself, stilled by his own stillness, and slowly he stood up. He had no desire to take a drink. He looked at the wreckage of the display with neutrality - someone else could drink the stuff and that was fine, it was up to them - but it wasn't for him.

Besides, he thought, he'd never be a customer here anyway. The shop floor standards were appalling.

He threw his bike in the back of the van and drove home. He lugged the food in, case by case, and stashed it in the basement. His employers, he was sure, would be delighted to know how absolute his commitment was to customer service. He really went the extra mile. Even after the end of the world, he still delivered.

He sat in the kitchen to get his breath back, then he walked down the hill to the church on the Oldham Road. It was near time for the Sunday lunchtime meeting, and he had to open it up. If he didn't do it, and someone went there wanting help and they found the doors closed - just by not being there, he could be signing that person's death warrant. Besides, he needed to be there himself. The world might have ended, but it wouldn't stop him getting to meetings.

He put out a block of tables in the middle of the room, then he unstacked chairs and set them round the tables. He put water on to boil on the gas in the kitchen, and he laid out coffee, tea, sugar, milk and biscuits. He fetched out mugs from the cupboards and spoons from the drawers. Then he unlocked the battered old wooden chest and he dug out the books, the meeting cards, and the pot for Tradition Seven.

He laid the books out round the table, one in front of each chair. He put the pot next to the sheets with the meeting format and the readings, and he stood the anonymity card and the serenity prayer on either side of it. Then he made himself a coffee, and he went outside for a smoke. He leant against the wall by the car park gate, looking up and down the road, imagining another person coming along - but no one did.

At five to one he went back into the meeting room. He sat down at the table and looked around the walls. He'd been coming here ten years, and it had never changed. The Steps and the Traditions hung together on one side of the room on their roll-down sheets. A4 slogans were blu-tacked in a line across the wall opposite. Take It Easy. Keep It Simple. Mind Your Head. One Day At A Time. Let Go And Let God.

It had worked to keep him safe for ten years - so please God, he thought, help keep me safe now.

He opened the meeting. He looked around the empty table and he said, "It's one o'clock, so I'll make a start. Welcome everybody to this Sunday lunchtime meeting of The Sanity Club, and a particularly warm welcome to any visitors or newcomers - well, I think we all know each other round this table.

"This is a closed meeting of The Sanity Club. Attendance at this meeting is limited to persons who have a desire to stop drinking. In keeping with our singleness of purpose, we ask that we confine our discussion to our problems relating to alcoholism, keeping our shares short enough to allow others to come in if they wish. Now I'll ask for a moment's silence so we can remember why we're here, and the still-suffering alcoholic within and without these rooms."

He sat quiet for a moment, bowing his head a little while he silently recited the serenity prayer.

God grant me the serenity

To accept the things I cannot change

The courage to change the things I can

And the wisdom to know the difference

Then he took a breath, looked up, and said, "I'm Charlie, and I'm an alcoholic."

He looked about the room and he felt the calm of it, the old church hints of dust and musty damp, the gentle weighted silence with its embedded freight of time and worship. Then he heard the knock on the door, so he got up and went to open it.

* * *

It was Luke. He wore his cream linen suit, and at first glance his outward appearance was much recovered. Still, Charlie didn't have to look too close to see the damage. He saw the slight, persistent trembling of the hands, and the way he tried to hold them steady and failed, and the way he shifted them to try and conceal it. He saw the skin collapsed into grey bags under the bloodshot eyes, and the veined blotches of red in the dry, chaffed complexion. He saw how his head shook on his shoulders, again that slight, just perceptible tremor, that ceaseless, metronomic shuddering to the inner rhythm of his pain.

Charlie remembered him - he remembered that snag in his memory, when he'd pulled up to look at Luke's nest under the viaduct - and an ugly string of images came swimming through his head. This was the guy who tried to make him drink. This was the bitter, angry creature who brought vodka to his kitchen. This was the demon who tormented alkies until one of them hung himself. This was the guy who hated us all because we wouldn't do what he wanted. This was the guy who came to end the world.

This, he realised, was the guy who lived in his head when his shoelace broke.

Well, he thought. Here's a test and no mistake.

Luke said, "I need to stop drinking."

Charlie thought about it, but not for long. The tradition at The Sanity Club was as clear as summer daylight - the only requirement for membership was a desire to stop drinking. And so, he thought, I better start at the beginning.

He said, "OK. If you've come here, there's a good chance you do need to stop drinking. None of us came here because we spilt a drop of wine on our tie. But it's not whether you need to stop drinking. The question is, Luke - do you *want* to stop drinking?"

"I do. I hate myself. I don't know what I've turned into. Everything in my life is just … it's just wrong."

"Well, that's a good start - and you're in the right place. I see you've cleaned up a bit too, since you were under the bridge there. Tell me, have you taken a drink today?"

"No. I went back to the Travelodge last night, after the world ended. The room's free now. I wish it wasn't, I wish we hadn't done it …"

"I think we'll leave making amends until later. I think we'll find you have a fair bit of work in that area. So anyway, the world ended last night? I've been wondering about that. Come in and let me make you a coffee. Perhaps you can fill me in. I seem to have missed it."

"What do you mean, you missed it? You were there. You were the first man into the fire. I saw you. You were amazing. That's why I want you to sponsor me."

"Whoah, hold your horses, chum. One thing at a time here."

He took Luke to the kitchen and asked him what he wanted to drink, and whether he took milk or sugar. He made him half a cup, so when he took it in his hands he wouldn't spill it with the trembling. He sat him down at the table, then he sat down himself and he looked at Luke and he wondered what to say. He wanted to shake him by the shoulders, he wanted to wring out every last byte of information. He wanted to beat him too, beat him until he bled and he was on his knees on the floor looking for his teeth in the dust. He was an alcoholic, he wasn't fucking Gandhi. He had a thousand questions burning on a mountain of anger - and yet the thing about the Twelve Steps was, somehow they pushed all of that to one side. Somehow, if you looked at another person and you saw that they were sick and you saw that you had to try and help them, then all your own stuff slipped away to the back of the queue. It could wait, and it would be alright.

"So," he asked Luke, "when did you decide you'd had enough?"

* * *

Luke had been drinking since they first gave him this region. It helped him blend in with the locals - but above all, looking back, what it did most of all was it took the edge off. The job was hard, he felt the pressure, he was chasing round scouring up souls off every rock and gas cloud in sight, the board were eternally on his case over sales, waste, shrink, community outreach, colleague development, marketplace positioning, yadda yadda yadda forever in your brainpiece, and obviously it was just good to kick back of an evening and sink a few. And of course he could handle it, couldn't he? He was Latest Model Demon. He made Blade Runner look like The Flintstones.

Then the order came down to wipe Earth. He knew it was coming, the experiment was always a dog's breakfast, human beings were a total nightmare. They were unfixable - resolutely, gigantically stubborn. The return on investment was pitiful. So he started planning it, he started spending more time here - and it did for him. His head just went. He couldn't believe how fast he'd gone into tailspin - but he looked at what he was doing, and he just didn't want to do it any more. Because who would? It made no sense. The only possible sane thing to do with the human race was to leave them alone and let them do the job for you. They'd incinerate themselves in a century or so and he needn't have lifted a finger. And then he started spending time with them, and ... he couldn't say. His heart just went out of the job. So he had a drink, and he had another one, and everything just accumulated on him.

"And then finally," he told Charlie, "there was you and that fucking playlist."

Charlie snorted with laughter. "You're telling me music made you drink?"

"No. I'm telling you music made me feel sorry for myself."

"OK," said Charlie, "I get that. But it does have other effects."

"Not if you can't do it. It was like, human beings can do this amazing thing, and I can't. It made me feel so useless. There are so many of you just not evil, you are such hard work - and as if that's not enough, you've got music as well. I tell you, I was lying there listening to Steely Dan, and I wanted to die."

"Oh don't worry about that," Charlie grinned, "that's a very common feeling. Not one I agree with, but it's widely shared. All the same, it doesn't explain why you've turned up here."

"I came here," Luke told him, "because I saw you and Molly die. But she's not dead, and nor are you. So someone around here has a lot more power than I'll ever have. In other words, I surrender."

* * *

Molly stood looking at the rubble-strewn crater where her house used to be. She didn't mind that it was gone - she had another place, after all - and it had been a good weekend's work. She had saved an entire species - one of the most interesting ones there was, for all the exasperation involved in looking after them - by the simple if somewhat hefty expedient of moving them en masse to another universe. She had frustrated the other guy in one of his more pointlessly murderous and destructive schemes, which was always satisfying. And she had, she suspected, greatly annoyed Charlie Fish, which might not strictly speaking have been a good thing to do, but which was nonetheless pretty funny.

Here he was now, stomping down the street with his grumpy head on. Absolutely typical alky - you save his life, and he gets a resentment over it.

What, did he want consulting first? Still, bless him, really he was soft as marshmallow. He'd get to where she was standing, he'd put his hands on his hips looking all wrathful, then he'd look at her and his anger would melt quicker than snow in hot sunshine. Which, sure enough, it did.

"Well," he grumbled, "you could have told me."

She asked him mildly, "Would you like me to have worn a badge? And what would you have said if I had told you?"

"I'd have said, Yeah right. And I'm Brad Pitt."

"See? A girl can't go about the place telling all and sundry that she's God. I'd have been locked up."

"I'm much better looking than Brad Pitt though."

"No you're not. But honestly, Charlie. There you were, flailing about looking for God, and who was there all along?"

She suggested they go and have a cup of tea. Obviously, she said, they'd have to go to his place - she apologised for the state of hers, but the devil had blown it up.

"So he did," said Charlie, "initiating in the process an electrical firestorm that was supposed to kill me, separate my soul from my body, and file it in a vial until they used it for fuel in the foundries of hell. Or so I understand. Unsurprisingly, I can't remember a thing. And, unsurprisingly, I woke up feeling like shit this morning."

"I take it you've been talking to Luke."

"I have. But leave him for a minute, just clarify for me - I'm not dead, am I?"

"You're not dead."

"So this isn't heaven?"

"No. This is Overtown. It may have its attractions, its burnt-out takeaways and its fine hostelries like The Dog, but heaven it is not. To go to heaven, Charlie, I'm afraid you have to be dead."

"Heaven'll keep then."

"You'll like it when you get there. Prince plays pretty much every weekend. Small clubs, big shows. Bowie less often, but it's not hard to catch him. Lou Reed guests with him now and then, when he's in the mood. And George Michael - what can I say? Flawless."

"I look forward to it. But in the meantime, where's everybody else?"

"Ah well. Now there's the clever part. You've heard the theory about the multiverse, yes? It's correct. Of course it's correct - what else would infinity mean? So there are many, many universes. Mintysquillions of 'em. And the good thing is, the other guy's stuck in this one. He hasn't worked out how to get to the rest of them. He's trying, believe me, but he's not there yet. So I've shifted everyone out of his way. Same human beings, same planet, different place. Just safer."

"That's genius. Is it exactly the same?"

"Not exactly. Mostly, but not quite. It's better mannered, at least for the moment. I don't suppose that'll last, people being people, but you can always hope. They still have to make their choices, which way they want to go - but if they choose to cook up hell again, they'll have to look themselves in the face over it this time, because there'll be no one else to blame. And then there's a few physical differences. I took some advance parties over there, ran some focus groups, we tossed some ideas about. Sadiq suggested the sky should be a different colour - that seems to be working out quite nicely. Me, I fancied changing the sea. I thought carnation pink would be neat, but I got shouted down. People said it'd make them nauseous, and they couldn't swim in something the colour of candy floss. Fair enough. I can always have a pink sea somewhere else."

"So what, you just clicked your godly fingers and off they went?"

"Hardly, Charlie. I'll have you know, shifting eight billion people to another dimension involves a fair feat of engineering. You have no idea. Literally. It's like creation. People say I did the job in six days, then sat about feeling pleased with myself on the

Sunday. Six days, ha - I wish. Evolution, for one thing - that's wonderfully complex. Don't want to big myself up, but evolution really does float my boat. And you think that took six days? Trust me, that one's so big I'm still working on it now."

"OK, fair enough. But what about me?"

"What about you?"

"Well - I'm not there. I'm here."

"You are indeed. Because I gave you what you wanted."

"You did?"

They were standing on Charlie's front step while he fiddled with his keys. He stopped and looked about him, up and down the empty street.

Absolute quiet. No people.

No quarrelsome, contrary, baffling, unfathomable people.

He thought, if he could just sit back and listen to music by himself - if he could just pray and meditate, if he could just read, if he could just lead a peaceful, simple life - if he didn't have to wrestle his head on every day just to go out and face a world where he'd never fitted in ...

"Yes," he smiled, "you gave me what I wanted."

They went in his kitchen and he filled a pan with water to boil it on the gas. She told him he didn't need to do that - the power was back, and he could use the kettle. Charlie asked, "Is that your doing as well?"

"Actually," said Molly, "I didn't do that. I have two friends I'd like you to meet. They've been firing up a wind turbine or two to get you back in business here. Or at least I hope so. Not been burning any carbon now, have you lads?"

Charlie heard a tiny chirruping, and saw Molly holding her hand out as if to lift it up and let a bird fly. "There you go," she said, "size up, boys."

Then she turned to Charlie and told him, "Give them a minute. Sizing up for these guys is a bit like a snake shucking its old skin, it's a bit of a wriggle."

Charlie saw the air start to shimmer in front of their faces. Something was growing there, at first just a couple of dots, then a glimmer from two patterns of light weaving about themselves, until finally two rectangular shapes could be seen emerging and settling out of the air into solid form. They were about the size of a classic iPod, but featureless. One was clearly old - matt black, scuffed, scratched and dinted. The other was shiny new, chrome and grey. The older one scooted through the air towards Charlie and a gruff little voice said, "Hi. I'm Binary. He's Quantum. We're big fans. I'm looking forward to hearing more playlist. Otherwise we'll be doing your engineering, we'll be maintaining your services. It's very nice to meet you. Oh, and the internet's back up. Thought you'd like to know."

"I did that," said Q, not wanting to be outshone here. "I did a media studies degree while I was at it. Took ten minutes. What a crock."

"Well," said Charlie, "that's fantastic. How cool are you two? Thank you so much, I'm so glad you're here."

"Yeah, but take care now," B told him. "We're evil robot spawn of the devil, so we might get out of hand now and then - but we're on a promise with Molly. We're going to work on being better. And torching the human race was just a terrible, terrible idea. I'm really sorry. I really am. I should imagine that really stung, didn't it?"

Charlie grinned. "I couldn't tell you. I have no idea. I have no memory of it, none at all."

"Best way, pal. Trust me, you do not want to feel your soul being ripped out of your body. You really do not. Spiritual waxing - not good."

"I'll bet it isn't. Thanks for the insight."

"You're welcome. So what's the next song then?"

"Well," said Charlie, "if memory serves, I believe Blondie are up next performing Picture This."

And he looked about him and he thought, Picture this indeed.

* * *

The boys went off to explore their exotic new locale - truly, they had never seen anything remotely like Huddersfield.

Charlie and Molly put their feet up. It was a mild evening, and they had the windows open onto the silent town - no traffic, no sirens, no shouts in the street. The playlist drifted out quietly into the empty world, a roll call of ever-changing memory and emotion floating away into the gathering night.

Charlie said, "You're going to leave, aren't you?"

Molly smiled. "You know I'll always be here. But this me, Molly Flite – you're right, she's going. She has places to be - whole other worlds. You wouldn't hold her back, Charlie, now would you?"

"I absolutely would not."

"Besides, you'll not be alone. You've got your two little friends - there's a management challenge for you. And I believe you have a new sponsee?"

"I do. That Luke - I don't trust him an inch though."

"When you stopped drinking, Charlie Fish, how many people trusted you?"

"Fair point - but I still reckon it's odds on I'll find him rolling on the floor at the Travelodge in a pile of empty bottles before the week's out. Moaning that he's from another galaxy and no one understands him and he doesn't fit in."

"Well, you should identify with him then - but as you know very well, it's not in your power to decide what he does. It's in your power to show patience and tolerance - so I'll leave that one with you."

"That's me told. Alright then - there's another problem. What if his boss comes looking for him?"

"He won't. For a start, he's so huge and toxic that he wouldn't make it past Pluto before the whole solar system was ash. That's one of the reasons he's so pissed off all the time - he can't go anywhere. He's had fifteen billion years to cool down and he's never managed it. I have suggested he chill out, but he really won't listen. So he's floating about in vast empty places shouting at people. Now he might send another of his serfs along, looking to find out where his eight billion went, but when they find the planet's empty they'll clear off. It's a numbers game to those people. They don't care about individuals. They're not going to turn on all that expensive machinery just to harvest Charlie Fish. So all I'd say on that score is, if you come across any serpents selling apples, have a care."

"Will I come across anyone else?"

"You will. Bless you, Charlie, do you really imagine you're the only alky on earth? Do you think you're the only one who chose this option? I can't leave here without making sure The Sanity Club stays alive. So you'll find over the next few weeks that a few more like you start rolling in. Off the top of my head, just locally, there's a farmer, a builder, a mechanic, two doctors, two nurses, and a conference organiser. I'm not sure how much call there is for conference organisers in the post-apocalypse setting, but she's an admirable person with a broad skill set and she's also a qualified scuba instructor. So if you all want to clear off to the Caribbean, you won't be short for leisure pursuits."

Charlie was thrilled. Unsurprisingly, being God, Molly had thought of everything. As for the prospect of a planet with no one on it but a scattering of alkies, it was both perfect and hilarious. A world peopled entirely by broody, self-obsessed lunatics with a truly dubious sense of humour - oh, they'd have such a good time. They'd polish their resentments, they'd take each other's inventories, and the conscience meetings would last forever.

"Wonderful," said Charlie. "And will we have to repopulate the earth?"

"I am," said Molly, "absolutely not getting involved in that one."

There came from outside, at first faintly but rapidly growing, a high-pitched buzzing noise, like someone flying a tiny, tiny model plane. Barely before Charlie and Molly could look up, B and Q came hurtling through the open window, one of them shrieking, "Rusty brakes! Rusty brakes!"

Two metal rectangles cannoned into the wall with a sharp clack-clack, then fell onto the sofa laughing hysterically.

"Ah," said Charlie, "the teenagers are back."

"Play us a song, Charlie! Play us a song!"

"Alright. Just the one though. Then it's bedtime."

Gotta Serve Somebody / Bob Dylan

"To be continued," Charlie told them, "another day."

* * *

Sadiq was leaning in the doorway of the store when he saw Molly cycling down the hill. She gave him a wave and came to a stop on the pavement beside him. She leaned her bike against the wall, and he gave her a big hug. He loved it when she visited - the world lately had seemed a kinder, better place anyway, but it always lifted another notch when Molly dropped by.

"So," she asked him, "how's life? How's business?"

"It's all good. The family's well, trade's steady. It's good to see you. All well with you?"

"I'm very well, thank you. The universe is definitely in one of its happy patches. Is everyone still OK with the new sky?"

"No complaints that I know of. I tell you what though, there is one thing that bothers me - just a little thing, but you might know. It's the papers. Every morning I lay them out, and every morning I check the delivery note, and every morning I have everything I'm supposed to have - but I still can't shake this feeling that something's not there. What's that about?"

"Ah," said Molly, grinning, "I wondered if you'd ask. Yes, that was a little bit naughty of me. The Express. The Daily and the Sunday - I lost them."

"You lost them? How d'you mean?"

"I dropped them on the way here. Just couldn't help myself. What can I tell you? Some things are so moronic, they test even the patience of God. So now there's a deranged editorial office floating in the void between dimensions, shouting about statins and house prices. Why, has anybody asked for them?"

"Never. That's a bit harsh though, isn't it?"

"Oh, they should love it there. No migrants at all. No Europeans either. Not one. It's the ultimate Brexit. I'll bring 'em back when they grow up. Anyway, never mind them. How's the Music House doing? Shall we stroll over and have a look?"

Sadiq's wife was behind the counter. He let her know where they were going, and they walked up the road in the sunshine to Charlie's place. The front of the house was clear, and an old car sat there by the kerb. One of the tyres was flat. A small queue ran from the ginnel down the side of the house, behind the car and a little way off down the street. At the front of the queue, one of Sadiq's volunteers manned the gate into the back garden.

The house played music. All the doors and windows were shut, and the music didn't actually come from the house - it was more as if it hung in the air around the walls and the garden, quiet and gently haunting, like an enchantment.

Sadiq had gone looking for Charlie a couple of times, when he first woke up in a world with a new sky. The second time he went round the back, and he heard the empty house playing songs, and every time he went afterwards the music was always there. It was something magical and he thought about it a lot, until bit by bit the right idea came to him.

He got together with a few friends and they tidied up the garden. They planted new shrubs and flowers, and they trimmed the little lawn, and then they started letting people know they could come and hear this strange, lovely thing. They didn't charge for it - they asked for voluntary contributions, and the money went to the reconstruction work in Fartown. Word spread, and The Music House became known far and wide.

"I miss him," said Sadiq. "He was an alright bloke. Is he doing OK?"

"He is," said Molly, "and he sends his regards. He's doing fine."

Charlie's Playlist

1936-1959

Cross Road Blues / Robert Johnson

Cherry Red / Big Joe Turner

Boogie Chillen / John Lee Hooker

Rollin' Stone / Muddy Waters

The Things That I Used To Do / Guitar Slim

Money Honey / The Drifters

Rock Around The Clock / Bill Haley & His Comets

That's All Right / Elvis Presley

Bo Diddley / Bo Diddley

Folsom Prison Blues / Johnny Cash

Smokestack Lightning / Howlin' Wolf

Be-Bop-A-Lula / Gene Vincent

Blue Suede Shoes / Carl Perkins

Brown Eyed Handsome Man / Chuck Berry

The Girl Can't Help It / Little Richard

Heartbreak Hotel / Elvis Presley

Please Please Please / James Brown

Bye Bye Love / The Everly Brothers

That'll Be The Day / Buddy Holly

Johnny B. Goode / Chuck Berry

Summertime Blues / Eddie Cochran

What'd I Say / Ray Charles

Take Five / Dave Brubeck

1960-1965

Spoonful / Howlin' Wolf

Money (That's What I Want) / Barrett Strong

Chain Gang / Sam Cooke

Walking To New Orleans / Fats Domino

Bright Lights, Big City / Jimmy Reed

Hit The Road Jack / Ray Charles

Comin' Home Baby / Mel Torme

Green Onions / Booker T. & The M.G.s

Surfin' USA / The Beach Boys

Louie Louie / The Kingsmen

She Loves You / The Beatles

I Wanna Be Your Man / The Rolling Stones

A Hard Day's Night / The Beatles

Not Fade Away / The Rolling Stones

I'm A King Bee / The Rolling Stones

Baby Please Don't Go / Them

House Of The Rising Sun / The Animals

You Really Got Me / The Kinks

She's Not There / The Zombies

Psychotic Reaction / Count Five

Pushin' Too Hard / The Seeds

Keep On Running / The Spencer Davis Group

Help / The Beatles

1963-65

Blowin' In The Wind / Bob Dylan

The Times They Are A-Changing' / Bob Dylan

A Change Is Gonna Come / Sam Cooke

People Get Ready / The Impressions

Under The Boardwalk / The Drifters

My Girl / The Temptations

The Tracks Of My Tears / Smokey Robinson & The Miracles

I Can't Help Myself / The Four Tops

Rescue Me / Fontella Bass

In The Midnight Hour / Wilson Pickett

Mr Pitiful / Otis Redding

Papa's Got A Brand New Bag / James Brown

I Got You (I Feel Good) / James Brown

Subterranean Homesick Blues / Bob Dylan

She Belongs To Me / Bob Dylan

Mr Tambourine Man / The Byrds

California Dreamin' / The Mamas & The Papas

The In Crowd / Ramsey Lewis

Drive My Car / The Beatles

Nowhere Man / The Beatles

The Word / The Beatles

The Last Time / The Rolling Stones

Play With Fire / The Rolling Stones

1965-1966

(I Can't Get No) Satisfaction / The Rolling Stones

Get Off Of My Cloud / The Rolling Stones

My Generation / The Who

Like A Rolling Stone / Bob Dylan

The Sound Of Silence / Simon & Garfunkel

Sorrow / The Merseys

96 Tears / ? & The Mysterians

Good Vibrations / The Beach Boys

Sunny Afternoon / The Kinks

Taxman / The Beatles

Eleanor Rigby / The Beatles

Tell It Like It Is / Aaron Neville

Get Out Of My Life Woman / Lee Dorsey

When A Man Loves A Woman / Percy Sledge

Try A Little Tenderness / Otis Redding

It's A Man's, Man's, Man's World / James Brown

Hold On I'm Coming / Sam & Dave

Ain't Too Proud To Beg / The Temptations

Reach Out I'll Be There / The Four Tops

Knock On Wood / Eddie Floyd

Mustang Sally / Wilson Pickett

Wade In The Water / Ramsey Lewis

Just Like A Woman / Bob Dylan

1966-1967

Paint It Black / The Rolling Stones

Under My Thumb / The Rolling Stones

Substitute / The Who

Paperback Writer / The Beatles

I Fought The Law / The Bobby Fuller Four

Ode To Billie Joe / Bobby Gentry

All Along The Watchtower / Bob Dylan

I'll Be Your Baby Tonight / Bob Dylan

Brown Eyed Girl / Van Morrison

San Francisco (Be Sure To Wear Some Flowers In Your Hair) / Scott McKenzie

For What It's Worth / Buffalo Springfield

White Rabbit / Jefferson Airplane

Somebody To Love / Jefferson Airplane

Break On Through (To The Other Side) / The Doors

I'm Waiting For The Man / The Velvet Underground

Sunday Morning / The Velvet Underground

Strawberry Fields Forever / The Beatles

Lucy In The Sky With Diamonds / The Beatles

She's A Rainbow / The Rolling Stones

We Love You / The Rolling Stones

I Can See For Miles / The Who

I'm A Man / The Spencer Davis Group

1967-1968

Memphis Soul Stew / King Curtis

Soul Man / Sam & Dave

Sweet Soul Music / Arthur Conley

Respect / Aretha Franklin

(Your Love Keeps Lifting Me) Higher And Higher / Jackie Wilson

Big Bird / Eddie Floyd

The Letter / The Box Tops

I Second That Emotion / Smokey Robinson & The Miracles

The Dark End Of The Street / James Carr

On The Road Again / Canned Heat

Going Up The Country / Canned Heat

Mrs Robinson / Simon & Garfunkel

The Weight / The Band

Parachute Woman / The Rolling Stones

Sympathy For The Devil / The Rolling Stones

Jumpin' Jack Flash / The Rolling Stones

Back In The U.S.S.R. / The Beatles

Revolution / The Beatles

The Pusher / Steppenwolf

1968-1969

(Sittin' On) The Dock Of The Bay / Otis Redding

I Heard It Through The Grapevine / Marvin Gaye

I Say A Little Prayer / Aretha Franklin

Chain Of Fools / Aretha Franklin

Son Of A Preacher Man / Dusty Springfield

Tighten Up / Archie Bell & The Drells

Dance To The Music / Sly & The Family Stone

Cloud Nine / The Temptations

Spirit In The Sky / Norman Greenbaum

The Ballad Of John & Yoko / The Beatles

Come Together / The Beatles

Lay Lady Lay / Bob Dylan

Space Oddity / David Bowie

Many Rivers To Cross / Jimmy Cliff

Cissy Strut / The Meters

Thank You (Falettinme Be Mice Elf Again) / Sly & The Family Stone

It's Your Thing / The Isley Brothers

You Got The Silver / The Rolling Stones

Monkey Man / The Rolling Stones

Midnight Rambler / The Rolling Stones

Gimme Shelter / The Rolling Stones

1969-1970

1969 / The Stooges

Cold Turkey / The Plastic Ono Band

Bad Moon Rising / Creedence Clearwater Revival

Lodi / Creedence Clearwater Revival

Who'll Stop The Rain / Creedence Clearwater Revival

Southern Man / Neil Young

Roadhouse Blues / The Doors

Peace Frog / The Doors

Maggie M'Gill / The Doors

And It Stoned Me / Van Morrison

Into The Mystic / Van Morrison

If Not For You / Bob Dylan

Big Yellow Taxi / Joni Mitchell

The Boxer / Simon & Garfunkel

Get Back / The Beatles

The Man Who Sold The World / David Bowie

Lola / The Kinks

Pressure Drop / Toots & The Maytals

The Tears Of A Clown / Smokey Robinson & The Miracles

Express Yourself Pt.1 / Charles Wright & The Watts 103rd St Rhythm Band

War / The Temptations

1970-1971

Get Up (I Feel Like Being A) Sex Machine / James Brown

Brown Sugar / The Rolling Stones

Wild Horses / The Rolling Stones

Can't You Hear Me Knocking / The Rolling Stones

Bitch / The Rolling Stones

Sister Morphine / The Rolling Stones

Dead Flowers / The Rolling Stones

Me And Bobby McGee / Janis Joplin

I Hear You Calling / Bill Fay

Imagine / John Lennon

Life On Mars? / David Bowie

Get It On / T Rex

Respect Yourself / The Staple Singers

Just My Imagination (Running Away With Me) / The Temptations

Ain't No Sunshine / Bill Withers

Soulsville / Isaac Hayes

Family Affair / Sly & The Family Stone

What's Going On / Marvin Gaye

1971-1972

One Of These Days / Pink Floyd

Won't Get Fooled Again / The Who

The Changeling / The Doors

Love Her Madly / The Doors

L.A. Woman / The Doors

Riders On The Storm / The Doors

Inner City Blues (Make Me Wanna Holler) / Marvin Gaye

Papa Was A Rollin' Stone / The Temptations

Pusherman / Curtis Mayfield

Use Me / Bill Withers

Superstition / Stevie Wonder

I'll Take You There / The Staple Singers

Love And Happiness / Al Green

Lean On Me / Bill Withers

1972

I Can See Clearly Now / Johnny Nash

The Harder They Come / Jimmy Cliff

Funky Kingston / Toots & The Maytals

Shine A Light / The Rolling Stones

Heart Of Gold / Neil Young

Peace Like A River / Paul Simon

You're So Vain / Carly Simon

Rocket Man / Elton John

Telegram Sam / T Rex

Suffragette City / David Bowie

Starman / David Bowie

Rock & Roll Suicide / David Bowie

Perfect Day / Lou Reed

Walk On The Wild Side / Lou Reed

Satellite Of Love / Lou Reed

Ladytron / Roxy Music

If There Is Something / Roxy Music

2 H.B. / Roxy Music

Virginia Plain / Roxy Music

1972-1973

Do It Again / Steely Dan

Only A Fool Would Say That / Steely Dan

Hercules / Aaron Neville

I Can't Stand The Rain / Ann Peebles

Let's Get It On / Marvin Gaye

Higher Ground / Stevie Wonder

Jesus Children Of America / Stevie Wonder

Right Place, Wrong Time / Dr John

Get Up, Stand Up / Bob Marley & The Wailers

I Shot The Sheriff / Bob Marley & The Wailers

Knockin' On Heaven's Door / Bob Dylan

Jolene / Dolly Parton

Long Train Runnin' / The Doobie Brothers

Incident On 57th Street / Bruce Springsteen

La Grange / ZZ Top

The Real Me / The Who

Money / Pink Floyd

Dancing With Mr D / The Rolling Stones

1973-1974

100 Years Ago / The Rolling Stones

Doo Doo Doo Doo Doo (Heartbreaker) / The Rolling Stones

Angie / The Rolling Stones

Aladdin Sane (1913-1938-197?) / David Bowie

Panic In Detroit / David Bowie

The Jean Genie / David Bowie

Pyjamarama / Roxy Music

Beauty Queen / Roxy Music

Mother Of Pearl / Roxy Music

Razor Boy / Steely Dan

The Boston Rag / Steely Dan

Your Gold Teeth / Steely Dan

Show Biz Kids / Steely Dan

Take Me To The River / Al Green

Lady Marmalade / LaBelle

Pick Up The Pieces / Average White Band

Just Kissed My Baby / The Meters

1974-1975

Papa Don't Take No Mess / James Brown

Fingerprint File / The Rolling Stones

Time Waits For No One / The Rolling Stones

Going, Going, Gone / Bob Dylan

Vampire Blues / Neil Young

Sweet Home Alabama / Lynyrd Skynyrd

Rebel Rebel / David Bowie

I Can't Hold Out / Eric Clapton

Rikki Don't Lose That Number / Steely Dan

Any Major Dude Will Tell You / Steely Dan

Barrytown / Steely Dan

Pretzel Logic / Steely Dan

Fame / David Bowie

Tenth Avenue Freeze-Out / Bruce Springsteen

The Night / Frankie Valli & The Four Seasons

Don't Leave Me This Way / Harold Melvin & The Bluenotes

Supernatural Thing Part 1 / Ben E. King

Cut The Cake / Average White Band

1975-1976

Love To Love You Baby / Donna Summer

Why Did You Do It / Stretch

Low Rider / War

Tangled Up In Blue / Bob Dylan

Black Friday / Steely Dan

Rose Darling / Steely Dan

Chain Lightning / Steely Dan

Make Me Smile (Come Up And See Me) / Steve Harley
& Cockney Rebel

Keep It Out Of Sight / Dr Feelgood

Teenage Depression / Eddie & The Hot Rods

Strangered In The Night / Tom Petty & The
Heartbreakers

Don't Fear The Reaper / Blue Oyster Cult

Hotel California / The Eagles

Fly Like An Eagle / Steve Miller Band

Don't Take Me Alive / Steely Dan

Cocaine / J.J. Cale

I Want More / Can

I Wish / Stevie Wonder

Golden Years / David Bowie

1976-1977

King Tubby Meets Rockers Uptown / Augustus Pablo

Have Mercy / Mighty Diamonds

Crazy Baldhead / Bob Marley & The Wailers

War / Bob Marley & The Wailers

Police & Thieves / Junior Murvin

Police & Thieves / The Clash

White Riot / The Clash

In The City / The Jam

No More Heroes / The Stranglers

Sheena Is A Punk Rocker / The Ramones

Lust For Life / Iggy Pop

The Passenger / Iggy Pop

Prove It / Television

Psycho Killer / Talking Heads

Paradise / Dr Feelgood

(The Angels Wanna Wear My) Red Shoes / Elvis Costello

Alison / Elvis Costello

Watching The Detectives / Elvis Costello

Sex & Drugs & Rock & Roll / Ian Dury

Uptown Top Ranking / Althea & Donna

Two Sevens Clash / Culture

1977

Natural Mystic / Bob Marley & The Wailers

Exodus / Bob Marley & The Wailers

Got To Give It Up / Marvin Gaye

Lovely Day / Bill Withers

Red Light Spells Danger / Billy Ocean

I Feel Love / Donna Summer

Europe Endless / Kraftwerk

Here He Comes / Brian Eno

Slip Slidin' Away / Paul Simon

Solsbury Hill / Peter Gabriel

Sound And Vision / David Bowie

Always Crashing In The Same Car / David Bowie

Heroes / David Bowie

Black Cow / Steely Dan

Deacon Blues / Steely Dan

1978

Picture This / Blondie

Teenage Kicks / The Undertones

Lip Service / Elvis Costello

(I Don't Want To Go To) Chelsea / Elvis Costello

Down In The Tube Station At Midnight / The Jam

Ever Fallen In Love (With Someone You Shouldn't've) / The Buzzcocks

Public Image / Public Image Ltd

(White Man) In Hammersmith Palais / The Clash

Hong Kong Garden / Siouxsie & The Banshees

Take Me To The River / Talking Heads

The Big Country / Talking Heads

Heart Of Glass / Blondie

The Model / Kraftwerk

Le Freak / Chic

Shame / Evelyn 'Champagne' King

Miss You / The Rolling Stones

Beast Of Burden / The Rolling Stones

Sultans Of Swing / Dire Straits

Gotta Serve Somebody / Bob Dylan

Acknowledgements

I started writing Playlist in Scarborough during summer 2016. I stayed at the Clarence Gardens Hotel, where Andrea and all her staff are excellent, and looked after me really well.

The bulk of the work was done in Hampshire later that year. I owe a massive debt of gratitude to Charlie Liddell for giving me a place to work, and to Charlie, Vicky, Will and Morag for taking care of me while I was there.

My love and thanks to Nic, Marc and Rachel for their support during the time this book has taken. I could not have done it without you.

I couldn't have done a cover design either. Many thanks to Jon Dyson for that last piece of the puzzle.

23313079R00183

Printed in Great Britain
by Amazon